SAMOIS

SHAKIR RASHAAN

publishing

Cover Design by Shakir Rashaan

Published by NEBU Publishing

Printed in the United States of America

ISBN 978-0-9986640-8-8

ALSO BY SHAKIR RASHAAN

STANDALONE NOVELS

In Service to the Senator

CHRONICLES OF THE NUBIAN UNDERWORLD:

The Awakening
Legacy
Tempest

THE KINK, P.I. SERIES:

Obsession
Deception
Reckoning

NOVELLAS

The SHEOL Corporation
Motives 2: The Drama Continues

ANTHOLOGIES

Z Rated: Chocolate Flava 3
A Summer of Seduction
Cougar Cocktales
Lies Told in the Bedroom

To my Beloved and my Beauty,

For being the anchors in the storm,

The peace in the chaos,

And the passion behind my pen.

ACKNOWLEDGMENTS

28 February 2018
0438hrs

Book number eight! Woohoo!

Look, I don't put them out with prolific volume like other authors, but I'm damn proud of having been able to get that many solo projects out with the other stuff I have going on. This one was probably the most difficult for me to write for a variety of reasons, but I'm happy it's done.

I'm very excited about this particular novel, and the reason lies in the gender of the voices of the characters in this novel. For those "in the know", Dominant women tend to not have a prevalent voice in fiction, and that was my challenge going into this project. I enlisted the help of a LOT of my peers of the female persuasion to help me get this right, or as right as I could get it.

One of the main reasons I wrote SAMOIS was due to a quote my Leather brother, Master Seykou always says: dominance has no gender. This is my contribution to help lend credence to that statement.

Okay, enough of the backstory stuff, this is where I get to be a little mushy and sentimental, okay? Cool!

To my Beloved, you were the primary reason behind giving Neferterri the voice and presence that she has. I know you enjoyed this as much as I did. I love you more than life itself.

To my Beauty, for helping to place your own essence and fingerprints on this project, there are no words to express what you mean to me. I love you.

To my mother and father, for the support that you've always

given me, no matter what the endeavor, I love you both with every fiber of my being.

To my sister, Rae Lamar, you're my ace, and my hero. I'm proud to be your big brother. I love you, girlie.

To my friends and family within the kink and Leather communities, particularly our LHOCC family: House of Blue (Mr. Blue and bluefrost), House of Nia (Master Seykou and luna), La Maison deRou (Master Mason deRou and kimi), and House of TREI (Mistress Choc and family).

Many thanks to the photographers who allowed me to use their names as a part of the story arc: John Crooms Photography, Andrea Garland/AS Garland Photography, and Solomon Abrams Photography/Urban American Gallery.

I also would like to thank the following organizations for allowing the me the same courtesy: Onyx Pearls, Women of Drummer, Women in Leather Legacy, and the HardPink Sisterhood.

I'm going to end this in the usual fashion because it's time to take care of the final lists before this thing goes to print, and I know I'm missing a whole gang of folks, so just do me a favor and insert your name in this next statement:

I'd like to thank _____ for the support and love. I hope to continue to put books out that you will want to tell your friends and family about.

Thank you for reading, and God bless you.

SPECIAL NOTE TO READERS

The grammatical errors that you might see within the dialog between the characters are not oversights. This is the type of speech and text that is used in some facets of the BDSM world. As one of my submissive friends put it, "The lowercase letters in a slave's or submissive's name are a demonstration of the hierarchical relationship. It is a reminder to the submissive that he or she is the bottom part of the hierarchy, meant to be led, and the Dominant's name is always capitalized, as He or She is the Top part, meant to lead." In keeping with the essence of the series and the essence of the BDSM community, preserving the speech was paramount. It is my hope that you, the reader, will understand and appreciate the symbolism.

SAMOIS

Prologue

NEFERTERRI

"How are the decorations coming along, Beloved? Do you need me to make arrangements with the landscapers to handle the grounds or anything?"

I was in the midst of playing ground traffic controller as I directed all of the movers and sub males who were helping with my new project. We hadn't been back from the islands for much longer than a month, but I was so hyper-anxious to get things started I almost pushed my husband and kids out the door at the first open opportunity. There was little time to waste, and I wanted to make sure that everything was perfect, or as perfect as I could get it.

Our daughters didn't mind too much, they were too busy enjoying the rest of their summer vacation before school started next month. Their grandmothers were all smiles, too, since they were able to do what they did best: shopping and traveling. This weekend's junket took them out west to San Diego so our youngest could play in Lego Land. Our older two girls tried to act like they didn't want to go, but once they saw the website, they couldn't get to the airport fast enough.

My husband was a totally different matter altogether. Ever the control freak, it took some convincing to get him to leave things alone. For the better part of the month, he was hovering over me, trying his best to insert "what he would do in this situation" to the point to where I almost banned him from my office. I'd love him forever, but he got on my nerves whenever he was like this. Thankfully, Amenhotep called to pull him away for a new project overseas for the next couple of weeks. I guess the old man could feel the tension whenever he was on video chat with us. I was so relieved to have my Beloved focused on something else, I had sajira and shamise pack his suitcases immediately. That didn't stop him from calling to check in on things.

"Everything is going along fine, Beloved." I fought the urge to roll my eyes and read him the riot act for still hovering so much. I realized NEBU was his pride and joy, but I wasn't about to demolish everything and start over, either. I had another plan in mind for something down the line, once the capital was freed up to accomplish it. If things play out the way I've planned them, NEBU will have a compound to rival its own extravagance. "All of the plans are coming together nicely."

"I know they are, I married an incredibly smart woman." He always had a knack for making me blush. "And that ass, though."

Now I really couldn't contain my smile. "You silver-tongued sonofabitch. I miss You already."

shamise and sajira walked toward me, noticing the phone in my hand and the lustful look on my face and realized immediately what was happening and who was on the phone. shamise took the phone out of my hand and playfully slapped it before kissing the back of my palm. She turned on the speaker so we could all hear the next part of the conversation.

"Daddy, we know You're missing us terribly and all, but we have work to do, and so do You. The last thing any of us wants is for You to get sidetracked. You're not fun to be around when You're not on schedule."

"Ooh, you're gonna get it, shamise." sajira giggled at shamise's brazen approach to their Master. "Daddy doesn't like it when you're being so…bossy."

"Yes, she will, but she's right, too," Ramesses remarked. "she knows how I get when it comes to large projects, but I also need to trust your Goddess will pull this off without any problems. I do trust it will work out fine, but I do get a bit…well—"

"Overbearing, Daddy?" sajira offered.

"Yes, baby girl, overbearing," Ramesses replied, pausing a moment before he returned to the call. "Now, your Goddess and I need to chat for a minute. I'll call you later when I've gotten to my destination and settled in."

I took my phone back from shamise to finish the conversation and get things back on track, waving them off as they tried to figure out what I wanted to discuss. I had to admit, though, it also gave me a reason to be nosey as to what my darling husband was up to. "Speaking of big projects, the girls and I tracked You by GPS, and it looks like You were flying over the Atlantic, toward South America. What in the world are You two doing down there? What grandiose idea has He got You roped into now?"

Ramesses chuckled over the phone, nearly breaking out into full laughter. I didn't see what was so funny, and the girls gave up looks to suggest the same state of confusion. He continued to revel in his private joke before he answered the question. "Well, I will say this much…once we're done setting things up in a few months, this will be a weekend event You, Blaze, Sin, and the rest of the Dominas will definitely want to miss out on."

"And what is that supposed to mean?" I hated when he insisted on being cryptic about what future plans were being plotted, especially when I couldn't yet be privy to them. "Eventually You will end up telling Me, so let's get that out of the way now."

"I'll explain in more detail when we get back from Rio, Beloved. I promise You will that You will like it, and it will give You an idea or two as to where You want to set up next." Ramesses paused for a moment as I heard words being exchanged in Portuguese. "We're about to make our final approach into Brazil, I will check on You when we get settled. I love You."

"I love You, too, and don't get too happy with all that scattered ass down there, either." I mentioned. "You have enough at home to take care of when You get back."

"You don't have to remind Me. I'll be home in about a week." Ramesses disconnected the call, leaving us to continue the preparations.

We went in search of amani, finding him and Jelani and tiger handling things near the main house. Seeing them all shirtless nearly caused heart palpitations from the three of us. Instead of interrupting them, we continued lusting from afar. It was one of the rare times we shed the titles and enjoyed being girlfriends. I made a mental note to consider doing something like this among the three of us more often. I had a feeling they would enjoy the reprieve to enjoy some things outside of the kink community.

shamise bit her lip as she stared at amani. "Are You sure

You want to let us loose as Tops this weekend, my Goddess? Like, for real, for real?"

sajira joined her sister in ogling the men, licking her lips as she continued staring at Jelani, Mistress Blaze's submissive male, one she was considering for her House. "Yeah, my Goddess is sure She wants to turn us loose as Tops this weekend, sis. From the talent i see on the horizon, it's going to be a very good weekend. i don't know about you, sis, but i'm going to take full advantage of this!"

I grinned, enjoying the visual of what was to come. "Yes, I'm sure, girls, and you might want to take full advantage of it. It's going to be a while before you're allowed the pleasure again."

We caught amani's attention first before Jelani and tiger figured out the reason he stopped working. I motioned for them to come over so we could speak to them for a minute before sending them back to work.

While I realized Jelani was still in his consideration phase with Blaze and I knew it was going pretty well so far, I found myself biting my bottom lip over how beautiful his body looked. It didn't help that the sweat from all that manual labor had his upper body glistening against the heat of the sun. I shook off the lust in my body and preferred to focus on my own property, who was now adorned with the same House crest pendant that his sisters wore.

To say I was proud that he was collared by us was a gross miscarriage of what that meant. If anything, he was worth every scrap of energy we'd invested into his training and development as a submissive, and I was looking forward to watching him evolve into embracing his surrender to us.

tiger took the lead in assuming his kneeling position the

moment he was within speaking range, with amani and Jelani following suit soon after. "Yes, my Lady, how can we be of service to You?"

"Yes, boys, I wanted to let you know I really appreciate all the hard work that you're putting in. I'm proud that My sisters have such dedicated submissives who understand what service is all about." Yes, I was lavishing praise a little thick, but sometimes you had to make sure their efforts were noticed. "Have the others been able to keep up with you three?"

"Yes, my Goddess, they haven't had a choice in the matter," amani beamed, doing his best to keep from blushing too much. "Some of them might not have a great word to say when it's all over, but at the risk of sounding flippant, we really don't give a fuck."

tiger laughed as he nodded in agreement. "See, there's hope for him yet. Got him cussing like a sailor and everything, just like his big brother."

"Well, keep them in line, boys, I'm counting on you to help Me make this work. If it does, I'll have something for you to run point on in a few months."

"Say no more, my Lady. Nothing would please us more," tiger replied. "Now, if You ladies will excuse us, we have a few more things to get squared away before the first of the guests arrive."

I watched them leave, taking particular note of the way my sajira and Jelani took special attention to each other. I had a splendid idea in that moment that would help my baby girl relax and enjoy her weekend and ease my own inability to help her get through this weekend. Not being around any of my submissives would be torture, but if I could find a way to make sure they were taken care of, it would help me run this event without any distractions.

If I got my way, I might be able to do that and then some.

Chapter One

"If you thought Ramesses was the only one capable of making big things happen, you've got another thing coming."

Watching the other Dominas' faces as they toured the grounds with me was more priceless than anything I could have dreamed of. When I first put the word out that I was planning a Domina-centric fantasy weekend, there was the initial skepticism from those outside of the Atlanta BIPOC community, with the usual criticism and doubt that such a production could exist, much less be successful. Hell, those within the BIPOC BDSM community were even more incredulous; after all, how many submissive men of color could there be, much less Black male submissives, and those of note were either already owned or had been placed under consideration.

At the risk of sounding like my Beloved, it was obvious that they didn't realize who the fuck I was!

Thanks to a few favors cashed in from the West Coast and a word-of-mouth underground campaign that swore every single one of the men who wanted to participate in this weekend to secrecy, everything had finally come to fruition, and on my self-imposed schedule. The stress and work was worth the effort, and it was going to be an interesting weekend, there was no doubt about that whatsoever.

A few of the lesbian Dominas took a slight offense to what I called the weekend, using SAMOIS as the marketing moniker, but I had to explain to them that the atmosphere was more pansexual than heteronormative. Thanks to my name, and that of Kemet-Ka, being closely associated with the LGBTIQ community due to the years of service and philanthropy, they decided to give it a chance, realizing that I was allowing transmen who identified as submissive and transwomen who identified as Dominant into the event, too. It was the first major obstacle I had to overcome, and it was something that was tricky to adjust to, not to mention it took some serious maneuvering to do so. I didn't want enemies off the bat, especially if I wanted to make this a yearly event, but at the same time, I couldn't make everyone happy. At the end of the day, they were happy once I broached the prospect of opening the island at a discounted rate for a weekend of their choosing, to smooth things over a bit.

Oh, since I have your attention, and you might not be completely aware of the reference, let me explain it for you as quickly as I can while the group continues to gawk at the eye candy I have scattered around the grounds. SAMOIS, or Samois-sur-Seine, was the city in France where the fictitious mansion of a Dominatrix in the *Story of O* was located. This was where O was sent by Sir Stephen to be branded and trained. The mansion was well-known in the novel as a location where Dominas were in charge, and the training and branding was done by the women. The men who might have been in house were all submissive; no Dominant men were allowed on the premises.

Sinsual and Blaze couldn't wipe the awestruck looks on their faces, especially when they got a good look at some of the men I was able to recruit. The beauty of social media was that you knew where the sources were coming from, and word of mouth traveled at a speed that made the average person's head spin. Between Facebook, Instagram, FetLife, and a startup social network called Chocolate Covered Kink, I had more submissive men than I could shake a stick at, not to mention ancillary access to vending and provisions of live deejays to keep things rocking the whole weekend.

The photographers were gracious in coming down to be a part of things, too. Having notable names like Andrea Garland, John Crooms, and Solomon Abrams on the grounds in case anyone wanted to partake in capturing their debauchery for posterity was absolutely boss. The moment the ProDominas found out they would be there, it was almost like the flood gates broke. It didn't hurt that I was a bit more risqué in the pictures I took with Ms. Garland, and with some coercion from the other ladies, we were able to entice those who were on the fence into engaging the event.

The Dominas weren't the only ones drooling, either.

"Baby, where in the hell did you find all this talent?" tiger did his best not to come out of protocol, but he placed his hand across his chest as he continued to ogle with the rest of us. He exaggerated the fanning gesture around his face, causing Blaze to laugh out loud. "I'm serious, my lady. I *know* these specimens are not all from the A."

Sinsual was not amused by his lusting over the landscape, but she couldn't avoid staring at a few of them herself. "Okay, Neferterri, where in the world did you find all of these beautiful creatures? I need to know your secret, because it's obvious that you've been holding out and then some."

I feigned innocence as I continued to lead the tour through the houses. "Look, all of this was luck, ladies, I don't know what else to tell you. But I will tell you that I'm not complaining by any stretch, either. Facebook and Instagram are beautiful tools, that's all I'm gonna say about that."

"my Lady, You know You're my favorite Domina and all, outside of my Owner, but with all due respect, You're full of shit." tiger put his hand out, waiting for me to give it a playful slap. He knew he was gonna get it from Sin the moment they were behind closed doors, but he had it in his mind that it was worth the admonishment.

"A lady never reveals Her secrets, tiger. Besides, why on earth would I even divulge so you can get your Owner to poach any chance She gets." I cut my eyes at Sin, the smirk on my face and the quick nod from my oldest friend confirmed my reasoning was solid. "If I want to continue to use My resources, then I will have to keep things close to the vest. I won't have a choice in the matter."

The rest of the tour went pretty smooth. I was able to showcase some of the things I wanted to advertise online, but with the current political climate we were under, it made that almost impossible to do without drawing red flags. Being in the Bible Belt didn't help matters much, but all that did was create other alternative methods of giving people an idea of what the weekend would have in store. One thing was for certain: based on the early turnout, there was definitely a demand for this type of weekend.

We moved up to the main house, where the submissives and slaves I hand-picked—including my amani—were on hand to handle the VIP guests whose attention I caught, thanks to some private conversations that were had behind the scenes. The six degrees of separation, even in the kink community, was real on some serious levels. Once they went through Dominic's vetting process, and their concerns over discretionary measures were satisfied, my designated valets were given the onus of ensuring that their service to those VIPs were taken care of.

A few of the submissives and slaves who were left out of the mix felt some type of way about being kept out of the special treatment, but that wasn't in my circle of concern. They were more than welcome to carry their asses home and really miss out, for all I cared. My brand, my name, was more important than bruised egos, and I was going to make sure my weekend would not go off without a hitch. If they played their positions instead of trying to be special snowflakes, I might have been able to rotate them in to relieve the ones who were in the initial mix. I guessed this was what happened when these "conditional surrender" submissives and slaves got caught out there with these Dominants that really weren't about this life.

Sigma, one of Dominic's security chiefs, greeted us at the door, causing the women to stop and eye-fuck the man from head to toe. The only thing he did was nod in my direction, his pace aggressive and measured as he approached the group. It took everything in me to keep from allowing his energy to overwhelm me. He might have been a submissive, but he also was a retired Lieutenant Colonel in the Marine Corps. There should be a law against a dark chocolate hued, six-foot-five-inch, hulk of a man that could make The Rock look small. Hell, even as delectable as the men in my life were, Sigma made me wetter than a tsunami, and I had no issues making sure he experienced every drop of it.

"my Lady, Your guests have been expecting You." The silky-smooth, baritone richness of his voice almost made me forget where I was and who I was with. "amani, Jelani and the others have been keeping them entertained, per Your directive. They're already raving and wanting to book a more private event later this summer."

Now, that was music to my ears. The VIPs in house were from the entertainment and political circles, and they took care of those who took care of them. I blinked away the lust, doing everything I could to focus on anything to keep from staring into Sigma's eyes. He was giving me all types of purpose and intent, and I wanted to avoid being greedy, despite the rumors Dominic started that he wanted to serve me in a more exclusive manner. "That is great news to hear, Sigma. Has the rest of your detail taken care of things on the perimeter?"

"Yes, my Lady, the women who were recruited from the Onyx Pearls, Women of Drummer, Women in Leather and the HardPink Sisterhood have worked out very well." Sigma continued to keep his eyes trained on me, but I noticed a nervousness in his body language that I felt the need to ease. After all, I wasn't the Domina to fear like that; that distinction still went to Sinsual. "If it pleases You, i can personally take You out on the perimeter so You can speak with them personally."

A smile crept across my face, picking up on the innuendo in his request. *He spoke to Beloved before they left, it's the only explanation for his subtlety in getting my attention.* "I look forward to that, we can do that a little later in the evening, once all the guests have been received. I still have a welcome reception to facilitate, and I don't want to disappoint the audience. Besides, as My head of security, your job is to be attached to My hip at all times, correct?"

"Um, as much as I'm enjoying this foreplay between you two, I believe we need to head

inside so we can sit down and partake in this welcome reception that You have planned, Neferterri." Blaze's voice was laced with a tinge of envy that I wasn't sure I understood. I snapped my head in her direction to make sure I wasn't imagining things. I came face to face with a scowl that threw me off balance. "Some of us have a few parties that have been set up, and we don't want to be late."

I shrugged it off, not wanting to kill the vibe in the air. My empathic senses were shooting through the roof as I did my best to "fix my face," as my shamise would often advise me when something wasn't right, but I had to keep up pretenses in the moment. Something was off with Blaze, and I planned to find that out before the night was over with.

In the meantime, I had a reception to take care of. There was no way I was about to start this thing off on the wrong vibe. Too many people worked too hard for it to fall apart on the first night. I wasn't about to let all that go to waste.

Chapter Two

Watching sajira as she moved through the crowd was a source of pride and lust for me.

She'd grown so much over the past year, especially after everything that happened while we were on the island. With everything that has been going on, I didn't take into account that there might have been something that she might need to talk about it. A lot happened, there was no getting around it, and after she recounted the gauntlet that she put herself through to purge, I wondered to myself as to whether or not it was actually out of her system.

I half-expected it to break her; hell, it would have broken me if I'd caught my ex-husband in such a compromising position with the "woman" he was with. As kinky as I could get at times when it came to Daddy, there's a difference when it wasn't negotiated ahead of time. It was a complete betrayal, especially when he was so hell bent on trying to use the mystique of the island to give the impression that he'd wanted to rekindle their passion.

I almost wanted to strangle him myself, but finding himself released from service and having to try to find his way back to the States seemed to be more fitting for his demise. He hadn't tried to contact her since, and it's almost a shame that he had all but disappeared from the kink community, although word on the street was that he'd re-engaged with the swingers' community. It was for the best, the way I saw it, but it seemed like his absence gave sajira the freedom to take her commitment to the House to levels I could only imagine for her.

So much other stuff had happened within between us all in one form or fashion; amani's relationship with both sajira and me had taken on their own poly feel within the House structure. I wasn't sure how it managed to get to this point, but the way he defended Goddess during that debacle with that so-called Dominant turned us on so much we'd damn near stopped looking at him as our "brother" and lusted at every turn over him. Even the relationship between sajira and me had deepened after she'd received her eternity collar; in my mind, it made things rock solid between us. We were in this together, for better or worse, putting in work to serve our Daddy and Goddess, for as long as the ethos would allow it for us.

I took a stroll around the grounds, sitting with my thoughts the entire way. I marveled over how things at NEBU had both changed and improved over the years. It no longer looked like an eternity of forestry when we first took things over from Master Amenhotep. Now, what was set before me was a swath of cottage houses, making NEBU resemble something of a tribal village complexity, with winding paths between them. The further into the dearth of the compound I walked, the more the energy of the tribe surrounded me, placing me into a surreal sense of serenity. I was home, in every sense of the word.

I continued my sojourn through the maze, smiling at the different women as they indulged with their bottoms. I couldn't hide my enjoyment of watching all the different kinds of kinkiness going on, despite the fact that I had to fight my own urges to want to be on the receiving end of the implements I observed being used. It was times like this where I almost regretted agreeing to be in Top space all weekend long. If this kept up, I was going to all but beg Goddess to whip me within an inch of my life once this was done.

I continued through the maze, finding my way to the edge of the perimeter of the compound, observing as the security personnel were on their usual sweep as directed by Sigma. Everything was clicking on all cylinders, humming like a well-oiled machine. It wasn't like we were going to be disturbed out here by a non-kink element, but there was no point in trying to take any chances.

I did my best to fight the urges swelling inside me, but I couldn't resist the heat coursing through me. The officers seemed to be preoccupied with the perimeter, so I sat down on the plush grass and slipped a hand under my skirt. It wasn't blatant enough to draw attention, but it was enough to stir my sex into a furor with as much haste as I could muster. Being out in the open was the aphrodisiac I needed to get off, and my fingers plunged deep inside as my mind began to wander into all sorts of explicit scenarios.

My eyes fluttered open and shut, but they were open long enough to notice one of the officers watching me as I continued to pleasure myself into oblivion. She did her best to keep watching the perimeter and keeping a watchful eye on me, too, trying to decide if she wanted to come over or not. A subtle come-hither motion of my fingers brought her into my space within minutes. As she approached, I spread my legs, exposing my freshly-shaved invitation to whatever I wanted her to do in that moment—and she was going to do whatever I wanted.

The moment I was in her space, she dropped to her knees, her energy responding to me as a Top in the interactions between us. "Forgive me, my Lady, but this girl couldn't resist wanting to be in Your presence. This girl would love to be handled by You before the weekend is over with, when she is not on duty."

I didn't know how to react in that moment, truth be told. I always marveled at how submissives and slaves bowed in reverence to Goddess, so to have this woman on her knees gave me a rush that I wasn't familiar with. I did know that I couldn't resist the urge to make her take the edge off until I could get back to the main house. "May I ask your name, love? I would like to know who to ask for when you are off duty."

"This girl's name is brandi, my Lady." Her eyes remained downcast, despite my urges to make her connect with me. I didn't want to break the protocol of the weekend, but this was a new connection, and I wanted to find out more about her. "This girl has been a part of the Onyx Pearls for the past year."

I'd learned about the LGBTQ Leather organizations from Goddess a while back. We didn't really speak about affiliation due to the politics that she chose not to deal with years ago when I was first training to become a part of the House. As quiet as it was kept, Goddess was a founding member of a sisterhood of Dominas, but since they weren't Leather affiliated and didn't include those on the other side of the slash, it really didn't take off the way the other organizations did. It didn't really matter to me; being unaffiliated had its benefits, giving me the ability to move the way I wanted to in the manner I saw fit. I didn't have the stomach for the messiness of who didn't rock with who and the other land mines that I didn't feel the need to keep up with.

That didn't have anything to do with my current situation, though.

I grabbed her face, forcing her to look into my eyes. She didn't resist; in fact, there was a look of pure relief on her face that I made her do it. Her eyes were transfixed, mesmerized as I guided her gaze from my chest, to my hips, and finally to my thighs, feeling the familiar heat begin to radiate. "Do you like what you see, love?"

"Yes, my Lady."

"Come closer, taste Me." The adrenaline rush I felt from being in such a powerful position was enough to have me climax before her tongue was able to suck my clit for more than a few seconds. I sensed her hesitation, which aroused a different emotion inside me. "I won't say it again, brandi. Taste My pussy, *now*."

The feeling of her breath against my pussy was amazing as she closed her mouth over my clit and sucked it with a sense of obsession I hadn't felt except for when sajira and I were together. I grabbed her hair, forcing her mouth to lick and suck where I wanted, each shock of pleasure setting my nerve endings on fire. "That's it, lick right there…suck on it harder…oh, fuck, you're gonna make me come…shit, don't stop!"

I wrapped my legs around her neck, holding her in place as I shook from the wave that was ready to claim my body. Before long, my hips bucked, my muscles clenched tighter, and I damn near growled into the night sky as I threatened to squirt all over her face. The orgasm wouldn't let me go, and my growls soon quieted, the force of my climax rendering me speechless. All I could do was keep my grip on her hair, desperate not to let the sensation leave me just yet.

brandi kept going, almost like she wanted to suck the very life from my body. I fought to find my voice again before she caused me to pass out. "Stop! Stop sucking, now! Fuck, stop it!"

She lifted from my legs, disappointed that she'd been commanded to stop pleasuring me, but she slipped back into a kneeling position. Upon observing the mixture of bliss and irritation on my face, she immediately dropped her head. "Forgive this girl, my Lady, she mistook Your encouragement to continue pleasing You. she got lost in the encouragement. she will accept any correction for her transgression as You see fit."

This whole interlude became more of a head trip than I'd anticipated. I watched as brandi did her best to contain her disappointment, a subtle rock back and forth letting me know she didn't want to get into any more trouble than she might have already had the potential to be in. I'd forgotten she'd left her post on the perimeter to indulge my desires, and I had to figure out how best to handle the current sequence of events.

"brandi, there is nothing to forgive, I should have been a bit more aware of things when they got too intense for Me." I caressed her face, watching her calm herself at my touch. Yeah, I could get used to this and then some. "Go back to your post, and meet Me back at the main house when you're off shift. We can continue in more private and less rushed circumstances, yes?"

"Yes, my Lady, she would like that, if she is permitted to

say so," brandi replied, lifting from her position to get back to her post on the perimeter.

I watched her hurry, noticing that in that moment, no one had been around to witness our tryst. I was relieved at that, not for fear that we would get caught, but more to the point to where we didn't get caught. I wasn't sure how I felt about that, since my exhibitionist kink is always in need of being fed.

I checked my watch and realized I needed to get back to the main house myself, or I would miss out on the opening ceremonies. I may have been in Top space, but I was not about to bring any type of dishonor to my House, under any circumstances. I'd rather die first.

Chapter Three

"my Lady, security personnel are reporting an unusual transport requesting entrance into the compound. Should I give the approval for entry?" Sigma's voice sounded a bit strange, which had me thinking I needed to see whatever had him so disturbed for myself. "She has the proper credentials for entry, but the mode of transport is…unusual, my Lady."

The thing about the kink community that most who are not fully immersed inside of it would not know nor understand is that we tended to have an extraordinary flare for the dramatic and theatrical. The extravagance of NEBU and the other compounds were the living embodiment of that flare. While we indulged in scene names and such to take on the alter egos we have, there were those of us who took that flare and cranked it to a whole different level.

In the city of Atlanta, there was only one Domina whose transportation would cause Sigma to struggle to find the words to express what was sitting in front of him: Mistress Hera.

I wasn't sure if I wanted to see how she would make her entrance this time. She's legendary for her over-the-top appearances at various locations over the years, almost to the point to where it became an expectation. She's almost earned cartoon character status, and I couldn't say whether that was a bad thing or not, but for the pure spectacle of it, I wanted to see what she might have come up with this time. "Sigma, allow her entry, I want to see this for myself, and I think the other guests will get a kick out of it, too."

"As You wish, my Lady," Sigma replied over the radio.

shamise and sajira walked up at the exact moment the murmurs began as they looked in the distance at what was approaching. sajira's mouth dropped, causing her sis to pick it up and close it, but even she had to admit that even this was a new and interesting entrance for Hera. "Goddess, is that…oh my God, it is. What in the world am I seeing right now?"

sajira was still trying to find the words to describe it. "How in the world…like, is that twelve of them? How did She get them to do all that?"

What my girls were struggling to comprehend—and something that I was sure Beloved would swear I was making up if I didn't have the security footage to prove it—was the sight of Mistress Hera in a horse-drawn carriage, making her way toward the main house to register for the weekend. The carriage wasn't the unusual part that rendered my girls and Sigma speechless, though. What had them trying to regain some semblance of understanding was the fact that the carriage was being powered by twelve submissive males, all in closet to full pony play regalia.

Quick lesson before we move on: there are those who prefer the term "bio-equine", due to the lengths they go to look like horses, most want to be regarded as such, as opposed to pony boys. Now that that's out of the way, let's move on, shall we?

Witnessing one bio-equine was one thing. A full dozen, all

harnessed up and prancing, was a whole other thing altogether.

Yeah, I needed a cigar and a drink after we were done watching all this go down. If I didn't know Hera any better than I already did, I realized that this was only the beginning of the production that was playing out before our collective eyes. As she got closer, I almost hated the fact that I was pretty much spot on with my assessment of the situation.

"Wow! She has twelve pony boys pulling her!" I heard one onlooker shout.

"Are you serious right now? How did She get that many to pull in unison like that?" Another person mused as we continued to look on with vested interest.

I shook my head as I watched these strapping young men pull her carriage with a precision that I knew took weeks to prepare. I took a quick head count based on what I remembered from the last time I'd spoken to Hera, and I knew for a fact that she'd only had four boys who were established property, but that was a year ago when that conversation took place.

Hera was no slouch for a woman in her late fifties, possessing a body she worked hard to maintain, making women twenty years her junior wish they could be like her when they grew up. It was safe to say she could attract these submissives to pull off the theatrics, among other things she might have commanded. One thing was certain: she had a type, and she stuck to that type with a tenacity that would make most casting directors jealous.

Her own boys were all over six feet tall, and the other eight didn't stray from that primary physical attribute. Beyond that, everything else was a matter of providing a smorgasbord of delectable eye candy for others to indulge, if she saw fit to loan them out for the night. The rules of the weekend being what they were, that meant she had no issues being in compliance. From blonde to redhead, from pale to tanned and everything in between, and from toned to cock-diesel muscular, Hera never disappointed.

All twelve boys were in latex boy shorts, knee braces and leather boots, no doubt due to the intense Georgia heat, otherwise I would have expected them to be in full body suits, head gear and hoof boots. My guess was she wasn't in a full-blown sadistic mood this weekend, but there's a fine line between sadism and outright cruelty, too.

We locked eyes as her carriage made it to the front entrance of the main house before she snapped the reins to cause the boys to stop. She gave a nod in my direction, to which I returned the nod in acknowledgement that she was nowhere near done with what she'd had planned.

By now, Blaze and Sin made their way to where I was, and upon recognition that Hera was on the premises, both women reacted with near identical indifference. Sin was the first to take notice of the boys in their gear and sighed. "It's going to be that type of weekend, huh, Neferterri?"

"Wait, it gets better, Sin," I remarked, finding a corner of the doorway to lean against like I'd seen the next sequence of events before. Of course, I hadn't, but I couldn't let the rest of the guests know that I hadn't. If Hera was good for anything, it was an absolute fun conclusion to the scene. "I'm just waiting for her to give the order."

"Order? What order?" Blaze was still trying to get over the divineness of the men still harnessed up, that was until Hera put down the reins and clapped three times in rapid succession.

Hera's property, the four at the front of the line, and the two boys behind them, unhooked from their bits and harnesses and proceeded to the side of the carriage upon hearing the clapping. Two of them dropped to their knees to await their Owner as she proceeded to make herself comfortable on the lounge chair that lay with the rest of the luggage she had for the weekend. The other four boys were meticulous in their duties collecting her luggage and cases that housed her various implements.

Once they were secured and a safe distance away from the carriage, Hera clapped her hands again. Hearing that signal, the other six boys unharnessed and began clearing and packing the bridles and harnesses before taking their places to the side of the carriage and guiding it toward the parking area. Once the carriage was parked, the boys dropped to kneeling positions, waiting to be collected by their Owner after she was done with registration and check-in.

Hera, meanwhile, was being carried up the stairs, as was her custom whenever she attended an event on the first day. She never allowed her feet to touch the ground until she was in the comfort of her accommodations. After that, all bets were off, but that was part of her quirkiness, such that endeared her to the kink community.

She raised her hand in a silent command for her boys to stop so she could exchange pleasantries. "Lady Neferterri, I'm so happy that You were able to put together what is sure to be a wonderful weekend of debauchery. I was almost prepared to return home when we were held up at the gate, I wasn't sure if You would have extended the indulgence I'm accustomed to. After all, we didn't get the chance to speak about it when I confirmed My attendance."

The smile on my face was genuine, as I held no animosity

toward Hera in any shape or form. It only helped to enhance the type of fun and shenanigans that the rest of the attendees would come to expect. "It was My pleasure, my Lady, the rest of the guests are buzzing over Your entrance. I'm sure it will be one of the talks of social media for sure."

Hera frowned for a moment, unsure of how to take my response. "I was assured that there would be no cell phone usage during the weekend except for emergencies, Neferterri. Is that not the case?"

I waved her off, encouraging her to take a look around and notice the lack of smartphones in the area. "Cell phone usage is restricted to the guest's accommodations only, as You can see for Yourself, my Lady. However, I cannot speak for the verbal accounts via status messages and things like that. If anything, it will definitely have You trending, which would be good for securing more talent for elaborate scenes in the future, don't You think?"

A smile crept across her face, as appealing to her vanity was the key to assuaging her and the discomfort over being caught on video. Except for the security cameras on the premises, there would be no threat of exposure that I didn't want to have happen this weekend. Besides, we had a reputation to live up to, also. "Yes, I believe You are right. Well, allow Me to get to registration, I wouldn't want to wear My property out before we get to our space. I look forward to a fireside chat sometime this weekend, yes?"

"I look forward to it, my Lady." We watched as she headed inside to the registration area, admiring the strength and precision of the boys handling her and her bags with the utmost care.

Now that the show was over, I had other things to take care

of. shamise and sajira were still at my side, ogling the eye candy as it continued its collective trek to take Hera where she needed to go. I laughed as I grabbed their hands to guide them away from the source of their temporary lust so we could continue greeting the guests who were still streaming into the compound. I only wished that amani was able to see it, too, but he was otherwise handling the VIP clientele for the next couple of hours. I didn't worry myself too much about it, he would be able to observe for the entire weekend to enhance and deepen his surrender to me soon enough.

It was shaping up to be a great weekend, if everyone continued to trail in with the frequency we were enjoying this first night. I couldn't wait to see what the rest of the weekend held in store. If this latest spectacle was any indication, it could have the potential to be epic!

Chapter Four

NEFERTERRI

I felt the need to get my girls in the proper headspace before the event began to overtake my ability to keep up with them. At the same time, I needed to make sure my baby boy was in a good headspace, too. It would be the first time that he would be away from me, and I needed to make sure that he would understand that this was an anomaly, not the norm.

I wanted to handle them in bracketed conversations, so I figured handling the girls would be the easier of the two to work through. They'd been around me the longest, and I knew they would be able to handle a couple of days a little better than their little brother. The way that I'd planned it out, including some surprises I'd had for them waiting in the cottage I'd had a specific crew of submissives to set up for me, would more than make up for things.

The girls met me at the cottage on schedule, and as I thought, they were a bit confused over the nature of my needing to see them without amani. The specific instructions were to step out of their Top space for a few moments so I could take care of my girls before putting them back in their Top space and carrying on with the weekend.

sajira, in her typical teenaged manner when she's around me, had to figure out the questions in her head. "Hi, Goddess, i miss You so much! Why are we here? What's going on? Why isn't amani here? Is something wrong?"

shamise couldn't stop laughing. Being the big sis, she'd had to be the more mature one, but I could tell she was as happy to see me in her comfort zone of being in surrender as her little sis was. "Come on, sis, Goddess has something up Her sleeve, and it's a good bet that it has something to do with our temporary new roles this weekend."

"I hate it when you can read Me, shamise." I let them into the cottage, waiting for the collective gasp to come from both of them. "If I'm going to have the two of you in Top space, I figured you might need to have the proper equipment. I can't have My girls looking ill-prepared."

"Goddess! Oh, my goodness, look at all this?!"

I smiled as I watched my girls start running through the cottage full of different implements and rope and chains and all the pretty "instruments of ass destruction" that my Beloved coined as a phrase so many years ago. Floggers, crops, paddles, whatever they could get their hands on, they could have access to. It was my special gift to them to let them know that it was going to be a very interesting weekend for them.

Now, let me take this time to sit you down for a minute, dear reader, so I can try to explain this to you as best as I possibly can without ruining the flow of the story for you, okay?

Over the past few years, Ramesses and I have been training our girls—shamise more so than sajira—to be Tops with regard to performing public scenes. shamise has been chomping at the bit to evolve into more of a switch headspace, but she never once wanted to step away from her alignment of her will to ours. Ramesses first noticed it during the special gathering on the Island, and between conferences and events, we sat down with her to ensure that she was ready for the responsibility of being a Top. She was insistent that she was ready for the prospect, and we rolled with it, giving her more responsibility in other aspects of House affairs.

sajira, on the other hand, wasn't sure if she was ready to handle it or not, but she wanted to be like her big sis so much that she followed right along with it. As quiet as it is kept, sajira was about as aggressive away from her surrender to us as any submissive we'd ever had. In fact, when we were all in the swinger community, sajira was quite the predator, stalking her unsuspecting prey with the skill of a ninja. That was how she got her nickname, Kitana; she reminded people of the Mortal Kombat character of the same name. We told her that she did not have to be like her sister, but we would support her if she decided to take that similar path.

"So, what do you think, girls? Will this work for you?"

shamise couldn't stop bouncing as she pulled twin suede floggers and placed them into the toy bag I set out for them with the utmost care. "Oh, this will work and then some!"

sajira blushed as she caressed the bullwhip in her hands, making me wonder if she was reminiscing over a few play scenes she'd subjected herself to. "Goddess…are You sure about this? i feel like i need to bend over a spanking bench at the first available opportunity."

I moved over to where she stood and gave her a consoling hug. "If you're really not up to it, let Me know, and I can have you join Daddy down in Brazil. I'm sure He could use the company—and a bodyguard."

She looked into my eyes like she'd disappointed me. She

shook her head, making sure I understood where her intentions were. "No, Goddess, i want to be here. To be honest, i'm curious about whether i still have what it takes to be the aggressor. It's just—oh, my God, it feels so good against my skin—i don't want to be a disappointment to the House."

"Come on, sis, it's not like i have a lot of practice doing this, either," shamise interjected. "Am i freaked out about this weekend? Like Daddy loves to say, "man, listen"! But i want to see what it feels like to be on the other side for a little while, and then i can tuck myself safely away once it is all over and be one of the submissive princesses of the House of Kemet-Ka."

Listening to her sis caused a giggle. I felt her relax in my arms, seeming to take the stress away from her. "That's My girl. Do you feel better about things now?"

"Yes, Goddess."

"Good girl, now do Me a favor and take care of your bags while I go and find your brother. I have to get his head together, too. I have a bad feeling that things are going to get crazy, and I need his mind clear and solid."

Chapter Five

AMANI

"I will be sure to tell your Goddess how much I have enjoyed your servitude this evening, amani. you are a credit to Her training and guidance, indeed."

Hearing those words were nothing short of magical for me as I continued to clean up from the massage therapy I provided to one of Goddess's VIP clientele, Lady Hatshepsut. It was a pleasure on more levels than I could count, but the most important was that I could make my Domina look stellar. It was no secret that my submissive sisters had more experience than I did, and I wasn't as well-known as they were, although the situation on the island sort of changed things a little bit. To say I became a pseudo-celebrity overnight didn't give the type of attention I received its purest justice.

Lady Hatshepsut was so well put together for a woman in her fifties that it defied all manner of logic. I was speechless when she disrobed for her massage therapy session, convinced that she kept up a fitness regimen that ensured that every asset she possessed remained taut and firm. As tough as it was to keep from being aroused during the session, I managed to keep my urges under control, despite the satisfied moans emanating from her lips confirming that I was successful in my initial mission of relaxing her from such a long flight and subsequent car ride to the compound. To have had the ability to provide service while her slave, senmut, was elsewhere as part of the rules of the weekend only enhanced the pride I felt.

"Thank You, my Lady, it will please my Goddess to hear that You were pleased with me." I tried not to lust over her, but it was futile and then some. Her body was gorgeous. "Is there anything You require before i take care of my next client?"

She caught me staring while I continued to pack my bag, slipping into my personal space. The scent of the oils mixed with the strawberry body spray she'd applied before she draped a robe around her svelte frame had me in a mood to where, if I wasn't already taken, I would have surrendered to her in a heartbeat. I realized it would be the case the majority of the weekend with a lot of the Dominas who would be attending, but if I didn't keep my wits about me, I would find myself in a few predicaments that would have me punished for at least the next month if I got caught.

"Well, pretty boy, this weekend is meant to indulge in a few fantasies with no questions asked." She stroked my face, causing shivers to roll down my spine. I closed my eyes as she leaned in close enough to whisper in my ear. "If I claim you during the Marketplace session, I'm sure I can come up with some delicious ideas. If I have to give up My property to keep things fair, then all's fair in lust and kink, isn't it?"

I gave up a half-smile as I willed my body to calm down so I could leave without being so damned obvious to the other women I passed on the way to my next client. She was right about one thing: whomever claimed me, I would have to surrender for the remainder of the weekend, to indulge in whatever kink she enjoyed, as long as it didn't clash with my hard limits. "Yes, my Lady, this is true. May i be released from service so that i may get to my next client?"

"Yes, you are released from service. I look forward to seeing you on full display later tonight." Lady Hatshepsut placed her hand out for me to kiss her palm before taking my leave, letting out a sigh as I turned to head out the door.

I made my way out of the main estate, taking a left toward the first cluster of cottages, taking a look at the directions on my note pad and the client I was to see next. I hated not being able to use my smartphone, I couldn't imagine what life was like before people had the ability to jot their schedule down by calendar and reminders. It gave me a new respect for the diligence my aunt possessed all those years as a private call nurse. I was ready to give up after the second appointment, chuckling to myself over sounding like a punk.

Realizing the cottage would take a few minutes to get to, it gave me a moment to reflect on the Marketplace period later tonight. That would be the moment where Goddess would release me from her control, albeit for the weekend only, but I didn't know how to feel about that. I talked about the separation anxiety with shamise, since she was temporarily released for more than a few months before she had to earn her way back. She explained it as the most anxiety-filled time she'd ever had to endure, admitting that she felt lost because her ex-husband pulled a bait-and-switch on her, acting like he could lead when he was more of a lackey than an Alpha male.

I wondered if I would have the same anxiety as I would watch Goddess claim another for her pleasure for the weekend. The other issue I would have to figure out is watching shamise and sajira as Tops this weekend, too. That alone would be its own adjustment, but I agreed to be a part of the festivities, so I had to take the weekend for what it was and find my own way of adjusting to things where I could.

Seeing a familiar face heading toward me helped give me a reason to remember that this weekend wouldn't be as hard to handle. "Jelani, what's good, bruh? Where are you heading to now?"

Jelani looked like he'd been ridden hard and put away wet, in the most literal sense I could muster. He was sweating and out of breath, and I noticed some scratches on his neck and shoulders. He took a deep breath before he attempted to answer my question. "Bruh...one of the Dominas...She wanted to wrestle...as part of my service...to Her. She's strong as fuck!"

I tried to stifle a laugh, but that was an abject failure. I doubled over, looking up at a confused best friend, wondering what I thought was so hilarious. "Look, bruh, i tried to tell you to be prepared for anything. These women are going to dump the bucket list out on us."

"Yeah, yeah, speak for yourself, bruh. It wouldn't surprise me if your Goddess tweaked your schedule a little bit to keep you from getting hurt or worn down too much."

I stopped laughing when he said that, flipping pages on my client list and the specific scenes they wanted to enact. I showed the current client I was scheduled to visit in the next five minutes and what scene she wanted to perform watched his face turn to stone. His eyes met mine, looking for clarity. "Primal scene and capture? What in the fuck is that?"

"I get to go out into the woods while She hunts me down, with a paint ball gun." I continued to work through the notes to highlight the "fun" parts. "Then, once She shoots and catches me, She will 'fillet' me like wild game and drag me back to Her cottage, where the scene will end. If i am able to escape and get back to Her cottage before She can either catch or shoot me, the scene will end, but we both know how this is about to go, right?"

"On second thought, good luck, bruh…and hopefully She doesn't shoot you in any sensitive places." Jelani let out a laugh of his own, and I couldn't be mad at him. At least he realized Goddess didn't make it easy on me, either. "Guess i'll see you at the Marketplace in a few. Don't know what to expect, especially when Mistress hasn't yet solidified things between us yet."

Oh, brother, that wasn't a good sign. He had been under Mistress Blaze's consideration period for the last six months, and from what he'd told me, things were going pretty well. Even Goddess was a little confused over why it was taking so long to move him into the training phase. If anything, it would have given him better footing coming into this fantasy weekend. The way the rules were set up, any property that was under consideration was considered fair game and if that property made the decision to be claimed permanently, the previous Domina had to respect the choice. To say this was dangerous territory was an understatement, and it had me worried for him.

I went for the obvious question because I didn't want to assume a damn thing. "Do you want to surrender to Mistress?"

"Keep it one-hundred? She's hesitating, and i have no idea why that is." Jelani shrugged, checking his watch to realize we were both about to be late. "There's only so much i'm willing to wait around for, and if another option presents itself, i'm going to see about it."

We tapped fists before going our separate ways, but I couldn't help but wonder whether I would do the same if Goddess placed me in the same predicament. Given the shortage of black submissive males who were willing to be out in public was a reality, who was to say that any of us wouldn't try to play the field a little bit?

I shook the possibility from my mind as I made my way to my next VIP client, getting my mind right to be prey for the moment—at least, I thought it would be for the moment. I would still worry about my boy, but all I could do was hope the weekend would provide a bit of clarity for him, one way or the other.

I reached my destination, knocking on the door to prepare for the Domina on my list. The name on the schedule gave a name I didn't recognize, but I also realized that I was still new and I wasn't supposed to know each and every person that had made it for the event. It'd been a lot of new personalities to work through and it had all been overwhelming to a degree. Imagine my surprise when my Domina opened the door, grinning her ass off as I struggled to pick my jaw up off the floor.

"Goddess? What are You doing here?"

"Seeing about My pretty boy to make sure he knows his Goddess is thinking about him."

"You're making me blush, Goddess. i've missed You, too." I did my best to keep my composure, but how was I supposed to do that when I was in such close proximity to my Domina? "i wish i could stretch this out longer, but i have to see the next client on my schedule."

"I know you do, baby. your next client is pretty demanding

at times, but I think She will be very happy to see you."

"And why is that, Goddess? i've never met this client before. Is She a good Domina to be of service to?" I continued to search her eyes, wanting to shirk my responsibilities for a stolen fifteen minutes. Anything to be in her energy. The flirting was killing me soft and slow, and I enjoyed every moment of the delicious torture. "Lady Hatshepsut was great to serve, but i know they can't all be like that. Are You going to be sitting in with this client? Did She ask You to be here, too?"

The anxiety levels I had were only going to ramp up to critical intensity. It was hard enough to put myself through these paces, but to have to do it with her watching with such a discerning eye would amount to abject sadism at its most cruel. I'd be so nervous that I'd end up doing more to dishonor than to honor her. The prospect was debilitating to consider, and I almost wanted to beg permission to rescind the session.

Goddess smiled, giving me all kinds of life as she touched my cheek. "There's no need to worry about whether you will satisfy this particular client. I know you will...because I'm your next client."

Chapter Six

SAJIRA

"I don't know why you're here. Isn't there supposed to be something that says that once you've divorced, that you leave your ex alone for at least a year or something?"

"Aw, don't be that way. Consider this a gesture of helping You to get Your mind right for the long weekend of being on the left side of the slash."

I was hoping to try to get a chance to relax a bit for a few moments before beginning this weekend in a headspace that wasn't exactly foreign to me, but one I hadn't occupied since—well, since I decided to enter my journey into submission, and since things went way left with the man who I'd promised to spend the rest of my life with. The unfortunate part was that he decided to flip the script and go in a direction I couldn't follow.

I'd heard rumors since we'd gotten back from the island that he'd been released from service by Mistress Sinsual since she was displeased with his adherence to protocol and his level of servitude to her. It wasn't like I was keeping tabs on him or anything, but little birdies kept telling me that he'd all but left the kink community, showing up at more swingers' parties than anything. I took some comfort in that maybe he had decided that he needed to be more in his element after Sinsual released him.

I was wrong on so many levels, I could have killed the "birdies" that tried to convince me that this particular lynx had changed his spots. If anything, it was a set up for a let down that I didn't want to see coming. Instead, I should have remained vigilant, keeping my guard up that he would try to find the right angle and time to see if he could catch me at my weakest.

Now this fool was in my cottage, on his knees in my bathroom, running a bubble bath while leaving a spread of assorted fruits and a chilled bottle of my favorite wine on the island in the kitchen. To say I was livid would not be indicative of the state of anger I was in. I was a level shy of creating a nuclear winter with the arrogance of this idiot being all up in my personal space. Someone was going to pay heavy for the bullshit I was going through right now.

First of all, I was trying to figure out how in the bloody hell he'd managed to get into my cottage like he had a right to be there, and then having enough time to get the wine and the fruit into the building, and do so without anyone being the wiser. Second of all, he wasn't even supposed to be on the compound since he wasn't invited nor did he belong to anyone who was an invited guest for the event. I needed to have a few questions answered, and Sigma was going to be the one to answer them.

"Consider this gesture unwarranted on so many levels it would make your head spin." I narrowed my eyes in contempt, irritated that I would have to burn some sage or something to ward off the negative energy once I removed him from my sacred space. "Now, as much energy as you spent in bringing this stuff in without My permission, I'm going to expect you to use that same energy to carry yourself and this stuff up out of here."

"What happened to You? You were never this…cold." The look on his face was one of abject shock. If he was under the impression that everything was status quo by the time we'd divorced, he was mistaken. "The woman i remember was never like this."

"That's because you screwed all of that up." I didn't want to have this conversation, but the fact that we hadn't said two words during the duration of the proceedings put us in the position we were in now. He wanted to have this conversation, then we were going to have this conversation. "The woman you remember betrayed my trust on levels that he should be fucking well aware of. First, you decided that you had to explore your sexuality without so much as a conversation as to how I could have possibly felt about it. Then, while we were on the island, you decided to flaunt that sexuality, to the point to where I caught you in the sexual act itself."

"You knew what it was the minute we got into the swinging side of things," he replied, his nostrils flaring up whenever I hit a sore spot. "All those threesomes with other men that we engaged in at parties, it never occurred to You at any time that perhaps there might have been a reason why i was down for the cause?"

His last statement felt like a bolt of lightning surged through me, coursing through my nerve endings with the force of the gigawatts a single burst could create. I felt almost white-hot with the type of anger directed toward him as I tried to process what he'd said. The idea that he was laying his bisexuality at my feet like it was my idea and I should take the fault for everything that happened in the aftermath was enough for me to vomit.

"Get out." I made my way downstairs with him in close pursuit. I didn't want him here, but I couldn't figure out how to make him leave without it getting any more hostile than it already was. I made it into the kitchen before he grabbed my arm to stop my movement.

His tone was calm, but tinged with agitation. "No, we need to talk about this."

"Leave. Final warning." A quick retrieval of one of the butcher knives housed in the block began to make my point crystal clear.

He held his hands up, his eyes trained on the blade the entire time. "sajira, wait, let me explain—"

I didn't bother waiting for him to say another word. A moment later, the panic alarm was triggered. Within minutes after that, Sigma and the security team closest to my cottage arrived, primed like there was a problem to be solved.

Sigma took a look at lynx before turning his attention to me. "Is there a problem, my Lady?"

"Yes, Sigma. This slave was in My cottage without My consent." My facial expressions conveyed that I was as unbothered as could be had. Inside, I wanted to rage and claw his eyes out, but I had to remain composed—at least until they left, anyway. "I wish to have him removed from My cottage, please."

"She was fine until i said something that She didn't like," lynx protested, giving the impression that he wasn't about to go anywhere. "i brought all this food and the wine for Her to enjoy. Does that sound like She didn't consent?"

I closed my eyes for a few seconds, feeling a full-fledged moment of rage coming on. I channeled my thoughts, thinking that Daddy wouldn't like it if I lost my composure when the situation didn't require it. I could hear him in my head, almost like he was in the room with me. *Think, baby girl; what do you need to do to ensure you don't lose your cool and accomplish what you want to have happen in this moment? you're better than this, My darling girl, and you're stronger than him. Cut where it will hurt deepest.*

It was in that moment when I smiled to myself; the response I needed flowed through with the clarity of an internally-flawless diamond. "Sigma, I admit that due to the preexisting nature of our former connection as My husband at one time, I might have given him some leeway with regard to his presence here. However, I did not provide him with any ability to enter My cottage, which means he received that access from someone else. I'm also concerned he might be an unauthorized guest on the premises, also."

"i'm not an unauthorized guest, i am still owned property," lynx stated, sounding disturbed that he was being dismissed with such ease. "She can vouch for my presence and attendance at this event."

Sigma looked at lynx, who felt a twinge of discomfort when he realized his defense was finding itself thinning out to near-nothing. He pulled his tablet out to take a look at the access code information and the person who last accessed it. He nodded before he spoke again. "Take the slave and remove him from my Lady's cottage. Leave the contraband for Her to enjoy, since the slave was being so generous to provide for Her, despite Her not consenting to the generosity. i'll deal with the breach as soon as we leave."

"Wait! This is unfair! i didn't do anything wrong!"

"The breach says differently, and your Mistress will be very displeased with this chain of events," Sigma remarked as he followed them out the front door. "Considering She is a NEBU Council member and you accessed Her credentials without Her knowledge or consent to pull this off, it will be quite interesting to witness what She might do to you. my guess is that it won't be pleasant."

"Wait, his Mistress? Who is his Mistress?" I queried, picking up on the last part due to my inability to get over my own shock over this incident happening. "I swear to God, he better not still belong to who I think he belongs to."

Sigma dropped his head and took a deep breath. My guess was that he was preparing for my reaction to his answer to my question. "my Lady, this submissive is still under the consideration of Mistress Sinsual. She rescinded Her release directive, provided he didn't screw up this weekend, which he already has by his actions this afternoon."

I was beside myself. Why on earth would Mistress Sinsual take him back, after everything that happened on the island? I sat down on one of the chairs at the bar and proceeded to pour myself a few shots of vodka. This was too much to deal with, and the wrong weekend to deal with it.

Before he headed out the door, Sigma stopped long enough to ensure that I was in one piece. "Should i get your Goddess to see about You, my Lady? She would want to be informed of this also."

I shook my head, content with opening the wine bottle and pouring myself a glass. I couldn't have her leaving to see about me and we hadn't gotten deep into the event. "No, Sigma, She has enough going on this weekend, and this was handled without further incident. If you would, though, I would like one of the masseurs to help relieve this tension."

"As You wish, my Lady. We will reset the login protocols to ensure this doesn't happen again. i'm not happy that this happened on my watch."

"I understand, and I don't hold you responsible. I have a feeling he was going to find a way no matter what you may have done to block the effort." I exhaled in relief as he left my cottage, peeling out of my clothes on my way to the bathroom—and the soothing hot whirlpool tub awaiting to take my troubles away.

Chapter Seven

NEFERTERRI

"Hi, baby, how is Rio?"

"It's beautiful, Beloved, we need to bring the girls and amani down here for a few days. Some time on the beach will do you all good."

I needed some time with my Beloved before this weekend began to get hectic. Seeing his face was a welcome sight; this was the first time I'd undertaken anything on this scale without him by my side. Between what I was doing here and now and what I assumed he was planning in Rio, this would be a matter of growth for the both of us. We'd always been a united front, even though he was only a silent partner with the club we owned.

It was going to be an interesting weekend, that was for certain. But I was ready for it, and I had a support system that didn't want to see me fail. By the time he would touch down Tuesday, I'd have one hell of a debrief to drop on him.

"Have You been able to find the location for Your event?"

The smile on his face confirmed what I'd already suspected. "Yes, Beloved, the castle is breathtaking, and it's out near Leblon Beach, so it won't be near the more tourist-heavy beaches. I'm not sure if Amenhotep wants to purchase it or not, but worst-case scenario would be a possible rental of the property from the realtor for that four-day stretch."

"Do we have enough liquidity to pull something like that off?" The accountant in me was curious as to whether we were stretching ourselves too thin. We were still pretty comfortable, but there was no need to be too aggressive. "What are the quarterly reports telling You?"

"The other investment properties have appreciated more than we thought, and some of the futures are promising, so we can move forward with some modest investments, but we don't need to do anything too aggressive." He nodded as he spoke, to remind me that he'd done his due diligence. "I'm more apt to want to rent and keep it moving. I'm not keen on spreading too thin outside the States right now. Market is too volatile for all that and we still have things to do with the properties Stateside to maintain."

"Okay, good, that won't be a problem. You know we have to ensure everything is working for us properly, especially since we've essentially retired, Beloved."

"Why do You think I took the private charter instead of going with Amenhotep's suggestion of buying a damn G500? He took one look at that thing and was almost adamant on buying it." He shook his head as he replayed the conversation in his mind. "I know there's money for it to be had, but there's the long-range picture that He has to be reminded of. I love that old man, but damn."

"Better You than Me. Beloved." I noticed he looked more fatigued than usual, but I wasn't sure if it was the jet lag or if he had something else weighing on him. "Are You sure You're okay? Your eyes look tired."

"I'll be okay, Beloved. I'm burning too many ends of the

candle. It's nothing a good twelve hours of sleep won't cure. It's almost midnight here, and My body is having to adjust to the time change." He rubbed his eyes for a few seconds, which only served to worry me a bit more.

"Why do I get the feeling I should have sent sajira with You? You better be taking care of Yourself or there will be hell to pay."

"I'm doing what is necessary. The last thing I need is for You and the girls to jump down My throat because I'm not doing what I would normally do when you're all in close proximity." He managed a laugh that didn't assuage my concerns as much as he thought they might, but it was enough to let him off the hook for the time being. "Kiss the girls for Me, and let amani know I'm okay, too. I'm sure he's in heaven with this particular format You've created."

"I will, Beloved. Be careful down there, okay? I know You know the landscape enough to be functional, but things are rougher than usual down there. Between the crime and corruption, I don't want either of You getting caught up in anything."

"This isn't going to be an extensive trip, Beloved. We're here to see the property and then it's wheel's up and back in the States before You know it. Dominic is insistent on it, He's more paranoid than You are about being down here." I heard the strength in his voice, despite the outward fatigue I saw. "I promise I'll make sure neither of us gets any ideas. I would hate to have to explain to paka if anything happened to her Master."

"Good, now that we're on the same page, get some sleep. Tell Dom I said hi and hopefully we will get the chance to see Him and the girls soon. I love You."

"I will relay the message, and I'm more than sure that Your event will be a success. You put a lot of effort into it, it deserves to take flight. I love You more." He turned off the video feed after blowing a kiss, leaving me to process the whole conversation.

I figured I'd get the real rundown once he got back Stateside, but I had a feeling he didn't want me worrying too much about things while trying to work through this event. I loved him for it, but he's as much a priority as anything. I filed it away as something I would grill him over once everything was said and done and take things as they came. Besides, he's never given me a reason to worry, no need in breaking that trend now.

Nevertheless, I sent up a silent prayer for Him to watch over the man who was as much the center of my universe as I was his. In my mind, it wouldn't hurt to have a little divine protection, and it would give me a sense of calm to take care of business until he returned. Once I opened my eyes, I was back in business mode, ready to take on this weekend with a renewed energy. It was time to put in some work now.

Chapter Eight

AMANI

"Sigma sent me, my Lady. he was concerned about You and suggested that i come to help relieve some of the stress from Your ordeal."

I knew my sis would be surprised to see me, but considering she did ask for a masseur to help with calming her nerves a bit, she shouldn't have been too surprised. Her smile put me at ease as I began to set up the table and prepare for her session. I had to figure out how to make this as therapeutic as possible, but we both knew that it was a possibility that other, more sensual entanglements could occur.

"Yes, amani, I wasn't expecting the situation that happened earlier, and it has Me a little tense and tight." She did her best to keep things on the level, but she couldn't keep her hands off my body. The towel that was wrapped around her body left little to the imagination, almost like she couldn't wait for it to fall off to give me a wonderful view. "Are you able to relieve some of that tension? For that matter, do you offer any "off the menu" services?"

Fantasy role playing was always a shared kink between sajira and me. It was something that we always indulged in, whether we were sexting to pass the work days away, or if she needed an interlude before bed some nights. I hadn't planned on the masseur-client scenario to play out on a real-time scale, but I wasn't about to turn my sis down, either.

This would be something new, though, since she was the Top and I was the bottom. I couldn't help wondering how that new twist would play out. "Yes, my Lady, i am a full-service masseur, as long as the client is happy with my services."

"Good, because I might need to be stretched in some rather compromising positions to get what I need out of this session." Her voice dripped with sensuality; the way she moved, it was coquettish, flirty, meant to entice me. "I understand if you're not supposed to handle your clients in such a manner, I wouldn't want you to get into any trouble."

"There's no worry about that, my Lady. The owner is rather liberal about the parameters of the session. As long as anything i do is consented to, She is happy."

"That sounds fair. The owner must be a lovely woman."

"Yes, She is. She can be a bit demanding at times, but the benefits far outweigh the drawbacks," I replied as I finished setting up the table. "Would You like to get started?"

"Yes, I'm all yours, just let Me know where I need to be."

"Sure, and would You please tie Your hair up for me? i wouldn't want it to get in the way of what i need to do."

sajira reached up to gather her hair, letting the towel drop to the floor without a single further thought. The moment she caught me gawking at her curves, she feigned covering her more intimate parts while winking at me. "I guess I shouldn't be covering myself, considering you will have to put your hands all over My naked body in a few minutes, huh?"

"my Lady, i wouldn't want You to think that i was a pervert

or anything like that."

"And if I wanted you to look at My body before you get to your duties?"

I swallowed hard, realizing she had immersed herself in her new headspace while taking the role play in an intoxicating direction. "my Lady, if You will please lay down on the table so i can get to my duties?"

"Well, you're no fun…at least, not yet." She laid face down on the table, wiggling her ass in the air as she made herself comfortable. "Maybe I can find a way to persuade you into a little fun."

She wasn't going to make this easy on me at all, but I was determined to make her work for it. "Do You have any particular areas that You would like for me to concentrate on? Are there any limitations that You would like for me to be aware of?"

"Well, I know that I'm tense, but there are no limitations that you need to be aware of." She caressed my hand as she guided it to her hip. "I'm *very* flexible."

"Well, my Lady, i do have strong hands, so please let me know if the pressure is not to Your liking at all." I grabbed for the coconut oil, taking a handful and warming it in my palms. "i want to ensure that Your experience is pleasant and pleasurable."

"Oh, I have no doubt that you will do exactly as you're told, sexy."

I moved my hands to her lower back, feeling the heat emanate from her skin, running my fingers up her back to her neck, retracing my path back down her back to spread the oil over her body. Hearing the satisfied sighs as she began to relax were a welcome aural presence.

"your hands feel amazing," she stated as I began a series of petrissage techniques, kneading through to the deeper muscles that needed my attention. Her body began to open up within moments. "I could have your hands on Me all day if you keep this up."

I lessened the pressure as I moved to the middle of her back, switching to a series of effleurage strokes, spreading my fingers to graze against the swell of her breasts as I used longer passes to cover more epidermal real estate to keep her from getting used to the rhythm of the motion. "How is the pressure so far, my Lady?"

"Mmm, it feels great, thank you for asking." She arched her back to meet my fingers and make me apply more pressure. The familiar "crack" was met with a series of moans and sighs, a sign that she needed to feel that release. "Oh, my God, I needed that so badly."

"Are there any other problem areas that You require me to work on, my Lady?"

In that moment, she could only manage a shake of her head to let me know she was in a zone, so I continued to work my magic. From her back, I moved to her legs, slipping my fingers between her thighs as a gentle request for her to spread them apart so I could work each of them without any interference from the other. I grabbed another handful of coconut oil, gliding my slickened fingers up and down her thighs, applying slight pressure to her hamstrings. I stopped shy of her butt, sliding each hand down her legs until I got to her feet. It wasn't until I began to work over her toes that I got a response out of her.

"Mmm, that's a weak spot, amani." Her coos threatened to make me weak, as I was already coming close to surrendering to my base impulses. "It feels so, so good."

"i'm happy to hear that it feels good to You, my Lady." I was going to hold out for as long as I could, but my body betrayed me with each moan that escaped her lips. "It is my honor to provide this service to You, to help You relax and take Your troubles away for a little while."

I continued to move my hands over her lower body for a few more minutes, using the petrissage I used on her back to loosen up the muscles throughout her lower extremities. I was careful to avoid her nether regions, content with the light snoring I heard from her. As a therapeutic masseur, this was music to my ears, and it was a source of happiness that I could provide my sis some measure of relaxation and peace.

Moving to her hips, I gave them a good workover, feeling the knots leaving her body with each application of pressure from my thumbs to those muscle groups. From her hips to her lower back, and back again, I continued to apply no more pressure then necessary to keep from waking her, getting lost in the massage myself as the service slut in me began to take over.

Satisfied that her lower body had received the care I'd provided, I ventured into the erogenous zones I knew she possessed. I grabbed another handful of oil, putting light work over her cheeks, kneading the left cheek, applying soft squeezes over her ample asset, moving over to the right cheek, alternating the attention to achieve the balance I wanted her to feel as I zoned out deeper and deeper into the techniques I was using.

I loved the sensations that surged through me as I watched sajira's body sway and gyrate of its own volition, a dance that entranced me. I didn't realize that my body had made itself present and accounted for until I heard her giggling for a reason I was unaware of.

"I knew I was sexy, but I had no idea I had this effect on you, pretty boy." She rubbed against my crotch, her eyes trained on the noticeable bulge that told us both that, whether I wanted to admit it or not, I was in the highest states of arousal. "I can think of a few things I could do with that."

"my Lady, as much as i want to, i don't want You to think that it was my intention to be so aroused around You. my job is to relax You."

"And you will...but first, I want to see what that mouth can do. I've been fantasizing about them ever since you came through the door." She lifted and turned onto her back, reaching for the back of my neck in the same motion to kiss me. There was nothing left; whatever defenses I had were broken. "Taste Me."

"my Lady, are You sure?"

"Yes, amani, and once you're done, you will carry Me to bed and tuck Me in so I can rest." Her directive was all I needed to hear. "Now, take care of Me properly, and I'll make sure the owner is fully aware of how satisfied I am."

Chapter Nine

NEFERTERRI

"my Lady, there is someone here at the front entrance who has a membership, but She is not on the approved guest list. She insists that She was confirmed two weeks ago, and has provided email confirmation. Please advise."

Those words gave me pause as I was chatting with Lady Hatshepsut and Sinsual and enjoying the environment. We were on the cusp of beginning the Marketplace portion of the night, and I was already a bit unnerved over how that could turn out, even with the added safeguard of the silent auction built in that Lady Hatshepsut suggested. Between that and not knowing where my amani would end up by the end of the evening only served to ramp up my anxiety levels to the point of irrational thought if I'd let it get that far.

"Sigma, who is the person trying to gain access?" I was in the dark over who the person might be, but the hairs on the back of my neck rose, which wasn't a good sign. "Everyone in the city was advised that NEBU was closed due to hosting a private event."

"Stand by, my Lady." Sigma paused for a few moments over the radio. The seconds felt like hours. "my Lady, She says

Her name is Norene Broughton. According to Her credentials, She has a verified membership to the Thebes compound."

My blood pressure, and my anger, rose quick. "Please inform Her that I will be at the front entrance to address Her directly."

"Copy, my Lady," Sigma replied before the radio went silent.

Sinsual was the first to speak, grabbing my forearm to stop me from getting up from my seat. "I need You to think this through, Neferterri. I know there is some bad blood between You, but I need You to have a clear head about what You're about to engage into."

Lady Hatshepsut nodded in agreement. "We are aware of Her disrespect toward You with regard to the things that were said and the complications with regard to Your amani, but we also need to exercise a bit of objectivity."

Objectivity? This woman all but called my ability as a Domina into question because of her female supremacist doctrine that a woman should never share power with a man under any circumstances. Add to that her blatant disregard for my ownership of amani and the designs she tried to have on him, and I was ready to erase her by any means necessary. That tired cliché of keeping your enemies closer was never one I subscribed to, and I wasn't about to employ it now.

"Objectivity is not what's on My mind right now, and with regard to the bylaws of all of the compounds, the ruling Council has the right to refuse entry during established special events." My emotions threatened to take control, and for once, I didn't give a fuck. "I don't want that woman anywhere near Me or My property during this weekend. I'm inviting trouble into My own backyard by even accepting the idea of it."

Sinsual took my hand and gave it a reassuring squeeze. "As much as You want to make that unilateral decision, You have to take the rest of the Council into consideration. That would mean Me and Blaze would be in on this decision, and paka would be involved with this decision in place of her Master. Lady Hatshepsut would be the tiebreaker vote as a Council member of the Deshret compound."

Blaze was quiet throughout this entire exchange, and that unnerved me more than this diplomacy that Sinsual was trying to exert. I looked in her direction and was even more disturbed at her indifference to my plight. I struggled to understand her neutrality, but I was more upset about the way things were beginning to turn against me.

Hatshepsut slipped into my personal space to get my attention. "This is not something that can be done lightly or with malice. While She has a membership to one of the sister compounds, what is in question is whether She was on the approved guest list."

I wasn't in the mood to be prudent or impartial, I wanted that bitch out of my universe. It was one thing to have an open weekend, quite another when I culled the list myself as invitation-only. "There is nothing in question, I invoke My right of refusal for this weekend."

"Neferterri, You're not thinking this through, You're letting Your emotions rule You," Sinsual expressed. "You'll open things up to a whole lot of unnecessary drama that I don't think You want. If it will help, we will head with You to the front entrance and collectively hear Norene out, that way it doesn't turn into a She said/She said situation. Fair?"

"Fair, I will agree to this adjustment." I stood to adjust my wrap dress before we headed to the golf carts. "But I'm warning You, if She so much as breathes in amani's direction if we allow Her entry, all bets are off, and I promise I will employ every measure allowed within the bylaws to bury Her."

"Lady Norene, we have some questions for You, if You don't mind the inquiry?" Hatshepsut decided it was best if she were the mediator to take the heightened emotions out of the equation. "There seems to be some dispute as to the validity of Your email confirmation."

Norene shot a look of indignation in my direction before addressing Hatshepsut's initial question. "I assure You, Lady Hatshepsut, that everything is in order with regard to My attendance to this event. I was informed of the event through My connection to the Panthers L/L organization."

Hatshepsut took the email confirmation presented on Norene's smartphone, looking over it with great care. Her eyebrow raised when she noticed something in the confirmation. "It seems this invitation belongs to Mistress Ylana, Ma'am. Is there a reason why You have Her invitation?"

"Yes, Ma'am. Mistress Ylana was unable to attend due to some last-minute business She needed to attend to. She transferred the invitation over to Me after we settled on the amount for the transfer." Norene kept a straight face, like she was sure of what she was saying. "There is no impropriety here, I would never do something like that."

"Can You answer why the transfer was not cleared by anyone here at NEBU?" I slipped my own inquiry into the conversation, not content with being a bystander. "Should we get in touch with Mistress Ylana to validate this transfer?"

"Mistress is out of the country, Ma'am, but I'm sure She is able to answer calls." Norene's demeanor seemed to be showing her agitation by the moment. Good, she needed to be uncomfortable. "Maybe we can check things against the final master list, just to be sure?"

Was she serious right now? It took everything within me to keep from strangling her on the spot. "Are You questioning the validity of the process when Your credentials are in question?"

"Lady Neferterri, please, let things play out, I'm asking You." Hatshepsut did her best to keep me from going nuclear, but it was becoming clear that there was some other madness happening here. "Lady Norene, allow us a moment to deliberate, if You please?"

Norene nodded, stepping away from the rest of the group. "Sure, take Your time, please."

Once we were away from her earshot, I made a call to the accounting firm I used to keep track of everything to figure out what the hell happened. Once they spent the next five minutes completing a series of profuse apologies, I was done. As it turned out, they got the deadline mixed up somehow, so they allowed the transfer of the registration, meaning I had to deal with Norene whether I wanted to or not. I should have listened to shamise and allowed her and the team she wanted to put together to handle it.

I disconnected the call, exhaling as I resigned myself to the reality of that woman being in such close proximity of my boy, among others. I was convinced she couldn't be trusted. "Okay, the firm I used to handle the registration process screwed Me, so, She's legitimate. Let's get this over with while I still have half a mind left."

I turned on my heel and walked with the rest of the group to reengage with Norene, who by now looked like she already knew what the outcome would be. I wanted to smack the sickening look of pleasure off her face. She thought she'd gotten the best of me, there was no other way to read her facial expressions.

Norene met my glare with a smirk. "So, I assume everything is in order?"

I gritted my teeth under the half smile I showed as I allowed Hatshepsut to answer her question for me. "Yes, Ma'am, everything is in order. We had to be certain of that, I hope You understand the need for the due diligence."

Norene's grin, to me, looked like that of the fucking Grim Reaper. "Yes, absolutely. I've even taken the liberty of bringing My own contribution to the event weekend, which is the plus-one in my registration. As You know, I had to release My long-time slave about a month ago, but I have a few in My stable who I can utilize when the occasion calls for it."

We were a bit confused over what she was referring to until the driver's door opened. Out stepped a man who looked like he'd stepped out of a health and fitness magazine. He walked around the front of the vehicle and dropped to his knees at her hip.

Norene patted his head before she made the proper introductions. "Ladies, this is karimi El, one of My charges. slave, this is Lady Neferterri, Lady Hatshepsut, Mistress Sinsual, Mistress Blaze, and Master Amenhotep's slave, paka. She is in Top space, per the rules of the weekend, just as you are a bottom, per those same rules."

As much as I wanted to be impressed by this physical

specimen, the fact that he was in deference to her made him that much less sexy to me. The other women, even paka, couldn't keep their eyes off him. Blaze looked like she was about to overheat, and Sinsual did her best to not make it look like she wasn't taking sides. But the specter of him being a switch was intriguing to say the least. That might provide the challenge I needed, and to stick it to her at the same time. Yeah, it was petty, but something wasn't right about her registration transfer, and I needed to get some fresh eyes on it.

"Thank You for Your contribution, Ma'am, he should make a fine addition to the Marketplace session later this evening." Hatshepsut reached to grip my forearm to give it a reassuring squeeze. "Please, proceed with Your charge and get checked in. We look forward to seeing You later."

The moment the car drove toward the main building, I gave each woman a cold stare. "If anything happens that I consider out of pocket this weekend, woe be unto anyone who gets in the way of My wrath."

"Neferterri, we understand Your disdain for Lady Norene, and I'm sure She knows it, too. She wouldn't be stupid enough to try to pull anything knowing the spotlight will be on Her the whole weekend." Sinsual tried her best to inject some common sense into the mix, but I wasn't having it. "However, if She does decide that She got over on us, know that I will personally help You bury Her, okay?"

"Her sentiments resemble those of My own, My Lady." paka gave a nod in my direction, meeting a reassuring nod in hers. "I refuse to let My Leather family down, Master would be very upset, and that is something that cannot be allowed. We got You."

I was still of the mindset that you didn't allow an enemy

into your backyard or you would live to regret it. The unfortunate part of that was that my hands were tied thanks to the bylaws of the compounds that I helped draft and ratify. I almost wanted to curse my Beloved, but there had to be a system of checks and balances to prevent situations where unilateral decisions like the one I wanted to make from happening.

I accepted the end result, but I damn sure didn't have to like it.

I decided it was best to keep this enemy as close as I could stand, but I also planned to have a few spies to catch her in anything that would give me cause to drop kick her into the next time zone. She could stick around all she wanted, but I was going to apply so much pressure that she would have wished that she'd turned around and headed back to New York.

I nodded in acknowledgement of their mandates, and offered my final statement on the matter. "I will keep My composure until I'm given a reason not to. That is all I have the capacity to do. For now, we have an event to continue to operate, so let's get to it."

Chapter Ten

SHAMISE

"So, i know You're supposed to be on the left side of the slash and all this weekend, but don't think for a minute that we aren't going to do what we normally do at the beginning of these types of events, girlie."

Having tiger in my cottage for our ritualistic paces felt like home for the both of us. It was something we began when I first got with Daddy and Goddess, and almost a decade later, we'd gotten to the point to where it felt like bad luck if we didn't do it. He'd been like a big brother to me, although he'd argue he was more like a big sister than anything.

"I know, baby, I was expecting you sooner or later, once the afternoon festivities were over with," I replied. "And I already know you have tea to spill, so let's get it done."

"Baaaabbbyyyy, listen! There's so much going on that was left over from the island weekend that it ain't even funny!" tiger was already on tilt, and I was there for all of it. "Remember that mess with sajira and lynx when she caught us together?"

"Yeah, don't remind Me, it took a few months to get her head back together before she filed for divorce." I shook my head over the amount of energy it took to get her back into balance again. "I'm still a bit salty over you not giving the head's up to at least give Me a chance to redirect her or something."

"You were too busy playing hostess with the mostest during the whole event for me to get to You in any capacity. Besides, You wouldn't have believed me, and You know it. Any who, it turns out that as much as he wanted to play the role like he was a virgin to the whole thing, it wasn't his first rodeo after all." tiger crossed his arms for dramatic effect, waiting for the proverbial hand slapped across the face in shock.

"Oh my God, are you serious?" In hindsight, he seemed to be a little bit *too* comfortable whenever he was around the bois during those submissive only get-togethers we would go to. "I'm not trying to believe that right now. he was supposed to be on the level, not like that bullshit with Jasmine when Daddy got kidnapped because she thought he was responsible for his best friend Jay leaving her for their former girlfriend, Candy."

"i know, that's what has me tripping, but it's been crazy, and it isn't the only thing that's been hellaciously crazy, either," tiger replied. He did his best to keep his own stress levels down. "Mistress has tried to get lynx right for so long it makes my ass itch. Anyone else, and She would have dropped his trifling ass before we took off from Nassau. i don't know what She sees in him. Outside of that body and that ass, he ain't worth two dead flies with his "version" of servitude."

"Well, that won't matter too much now. he's not in a position for us to worry about him anymore," I replied. "your Mistress released him, and he's gone back to the swinger's side of the spectrum."

I thought back to all of the things my Leather family had

been through over the past three years or so, and it was enough to make most people wonder how this House was still standing. From Daddy's kidnapping over the divorce his best friend was going through, to the situation with "granddaddy" Master Amenhotep and the trumped up rape charges from one of His former slaves, to all the madness that happened during the opening of the Island a couple years ago when the two Dominants tried their best to split Daddy and Goddess up for their own selfish reasons, it was a wonder why we weren't having our own kink version of the old soap opera, *As the World Turns*.

I even contributed to the drama with my own messy situation with my ex-husband and his transwoman mistress that I didn't know about, being stupid enough to force Daddy and Goddess to let me go, only to come back after all that and go through every hoop in the universe to earn my way back in their good graces. I mean, I got a few million for my trouble in the divorce to keep my mouth shut about his secret, but I was more afraid of what Daddy put me through than anything the legal system would have had for me for breaking my non-disclosure agreement.

"Umm, about that." His interruption in the flow of the conversation snapped me out of my thoughts and reminded me to rejoin the conversation.

"About what, tiger?"

"Mistress sort of rescinded the release order. That fool is on the property now as we speak." He sounded like he didn't want to explain that part, but there was no point in holding back any longer. "And before You say anything about not giving You the head's up, Mistress gave the directive to not say a word until She was able to talk to your Goddess and Mistress

Blaze."

I wanted to scream. I was sure he was out of the picture, and now we have to deal with his indecisive ass trying to sniff around sajira and screw her headspace up. I was going to need to get to her as soon as possible to keep that from happening. "So, will She take this weekend to observe him so She can see for herself that he isn't worth the trouble? I mean, sooner or later, the straw will break the camel's back."

"Man, i can only hope so in this particular situation, because there's only so much i can take with him." tiger sighed, shaking his head over the energy I imagined it took to deal with a submissive that simply wouldn't act right, no matter how much you tried to help them. It made me appreciate amani that much more. "he's a good lay and all, but i can get that anywhere, especially when Mistress allowed me to go through the paces with the Men of Onyx. Baby girl, them men are ridiculously fine as fuck, and the activism just sets everything off right!"

I couldn't stop laughing, but he did have a point. The ones Goddess knew through her connections with both the Men of Onyx and the Onyx Pearls were something to behold and then some. I couldn't wait until the next pansexual event we would be able to host or at least provide support to so I could ogle the fuck out of the lot of them.

"Well, I'm looking forward to watching what happens this weekend, especially with all the bois having to provide service to those who they don't belong to," I mused. "I'm not gonna lie, though: this might be my opportunity to see what's up between Me and amani, if I can angle it to where I can acquire him during the Marketplace session later."

tiger got quiet, something he never did unless he heard

something that made him want to pause and think. He looked me up and down a few times like he was trying to size up the words that came out of my mouth. "See, that's that bullshit i be talking about, sis. How You gonna hold out like we don't dish with each other every damn week? You got heat for amani?"

I tried not to blush, but I couldn't help myself. A lot of Daddy had rubbed off on him, and the residue had me looking at him in a different light altogether. "Okay, damn, yes, he's got Me feeling the heat. I mean, I know you've lusted over him yourself, so stop playing."

"Yes the fuck i have, baby, him and that frat brother of his." I watched as he took his hand to fan himself for more than a few minutes, trying to compose himself to continue the conversation. "Ain't that much fineness supposed to be running in twin packs like that, and it's going to be interesting to see who tries to break up the set later tonight. Someone is gonna snatch them up quick."

"That won't be a problem, and I'll be the first to tell you that, with a little tweaking of the system, they will belong to My sis and Me for the weekend." There was no way in hell I was about to not take advantage of a rare opportunity to handle some things and check off some things on my kinky bucket list. "If anything, I'll pull this off and make it all look like pure accidents."

"Look, i'm here for all of it, just make sure that You let me get the bird's eye view so i'll have something to take back to my cottage so I can go to sleep properly." tiger crossed his arms over his chest and gave me a look that dared me to forget about him in the aftermath. "This weekend was meant to be something next level, and i can't wait to see just how far everyone will try to level up!"

I was glad he was hyper about the coming prospects, but I needed to see about my sis. I wouldn't be right until I had a chance to see what was going on with her. If anything, I could at least give her the head's up and get her head together before she had the misfortune of running into her ex-husband.

The text from sajira almost made me jump out of my skin. *Sis, I need You. lynx showed up in my cottage unannounced. Please come.*

Chapter Eleven

AMANI

"Okay, sis, first of all, are You okay?"

"I think so. I'm still a bit shook over how it all went down. I thought he wasn't around anymore."

"tiger just told Me Mistress Sinsual changed Her mind and took him back on a provisional basis."

"Well, I wish someone would have given Me the head's up or something. That idiot was in My bathroom acting like the last two years never happened."

I was on the floor sitting between my big sisters as sajira continued to recount the incident, doing my best to refrain from asking permission to hunt lynx down and beat him to sleep. What in the hell possessed him to do what he did? And then to act like she was the one in the wrong was enough to have me go blank the minute I saw him. Whether Mistress Sinsual had changed her mind was immaterial, he had no business being within shouting distance of my sis.

I sort of came into the middle of the story, so to speak. sajira and lynx were starting to find their way on the outs, and my opinion of him had been colored by my sisters' opinions of him. Still, looking back on the whole situation, for someone who wasn't as invested as I was from an emotional perspective, it would be hard for them to lay all of the blame at lynx's feet.

The way I understood it, lynx tried to get sajira to offer to be considered by Mistress Sinsual, but she was already in the process of committing to Sir and Goddess by the time he'd decided for them what they were going to do together. After that, according to sajira, things were never quite the same between them.

From talking to tiger about it from his perspective, it was a match made in hell for him.

He had his own slutty tendencies, but he didn't think that his Mistress would consider him. He assumed that lynx was heterosexual, so that meant that he couldn't enjoy him the way his Mistress would. He was selfish like that, but he'd been with Mistress Sinsual for so long, it must have felt like he would have as much say in who would be by his side to serve her as she did. I couldn't have had that type of arrogance when it came to my Dominants, but I hadn't been around that long, either.

He decided to let Mistress handle the process with lynx, until he found out by accident that lynx wasn't as "straight" as tiger had assumed he was.

tiger tried him one afternoon at the house he and sajira shared as husband and wife, and shamise busted him. To his credit, tiger had told sajira already, but she didn't want to believe that her husband had made the transition into exploring his bisexuality. She was insistent on trying to fix whatever was ailing between them the best way she knew how, but that all changed when we were all on the Island last year. She got what she wanted, whether she liked it or not: lynx and tiger getting it in on the deck of the villa they were in, in broad daylight while she was looking for him to try and figure out things.

From there, it was academic. Once we all were back in the States, she'd filed for divorce, changed the locks, moved his stuff out on the curb, and all but washed every trace of him from the house before she put it on the market to be sold. It was swift, it was cold and calculating, and it was on from there. The next thing I knew, Sir and I became the men in her life, and the only men in her life, without a second thought or hesitation.

Hence, the reason I was ready to go complete Beast Mode and leave him without the ability to use any of his upper or lower extremities. "Say the word, sis, and we can reduce him to a shell of his former self without another thought."

"I'm not sure what I want to do right now, baby. I'm just confused over what I thought Was happening with My ex. He wasn't even on this side of the alternative world, I assumed, and now he's in My face, or at least trying to get in My face, at every opportunity, starting with that bizarre scene earlier today."

"Well, the only thing we can try to do is limit his access and availability to You during the weekend. he still belongs to Mistress Sinsual, so we're going to have to roll with the punches," shamise explained. "But he's going to need to be punished for the unauthorized access to Your cottage. Has Sigma and his team been able to find out how he got in?"

"Not yet, but I'm hopeful they will know something before the night is out," sajira answered. "All I want to do at this point is soak in My tub until it's time to head to the Marketplace session so I can act a fool the rest of the weekend and not even think about him."

There was a knock at the door, and I went to answer it, leaving them on the couch to await my return. I opened the door, noticing that Sigma was waiting. "Sigma, is everything okay? sajira mentioned that you were investigating something for Her."

"Yes, amani, and i have an update for Her, if you don't mind letting me in," Sigma replied. "i have a feeling She will be more than interested in what we've found."

I led him back into the living area where my sisters were sitting. sajira smiled at his presence, straightening up in her spot on the couch. "Sigma, have you found out anything from the incident?"

"Yes, my Lady, we have." Sigma took his place on the floor to present his findings. "It looks like lynx hacked into the system to produce the passcode into your cottage. It seems that he coerced one of my people who he somehow had some incriminating information on to give him access."

shamise was less than thrilled. "Please tell us that you have handled the situation and the person who leaked the information to lynx?"

"Yes, my Lady, the leak has been turned over to the proper authorities for the hacking incident, and I've alerted Mistress Sinsual with regard to the breach with regard to Her property."

"Is there anything that we can do to lynx specifically?" sajira asked. "I feel like I need him handled, but I don't want the messiness of bringing the authorities in. We would have to shut down the event, among other problems that could arise."

"my Lady, considering he has committed a crime of sorts, we would have to do our due diligence to hold him accountable. We would need Your consent to do so, but we will be able to handle it as discreetly as possible," Sigma stated. "If You would like to handle this a different way, there are methods we can employ."

I saw the wheels turning in sajira's head, and I wanted to influence her to take door number two so I could get in on the action. I also realized that she would have to work out the final decision without anyone getting into the mix to sway her. My issues with him weren't altogether separate from hers, but I wanted to handle them on my own time and energy.

"Sigma, no harm was done, to be honest, and I wouldn't want to have him arrested, but I want to reserve the right to handle him without any law enforcement influence." sajira continued to ponder her response. "I want to put some fear in him more than anything, so he can leave Me alone. It's becoming problematic seeing him pop up at the least opportune moments. I'm hopeful that he will be selected during the Marketplace session so he will be too occupied to worry about Me."

"As You wish, my Lady. We will keep him under constant surveillance, and if he does something to get into Your personal space without Your consent, we will ban him for the next six months."

"Thank you, Sigma, I'm happy with that compromise. Please let Goddess know that the masseur She sent was more than adequate in getting Me back on track."

"Yes, my Lady. She is looking forward to meeting up with You during the Marketplace session later. i will take my leave now."

Once he'd left the cottage, we got back around to the conversation at hand. I was a bit sheepish about the questions in my head, but I felt comfortable with them to bring certain things up to get their opinions on things. I settled myself back in my space between them and sorted through my head for the questions I wanted to ask.

"Have You given any thought to who You would like to have serve You this weekend?" My question was asked with a selfish purpose in mind. As much as I would have rather been both of theirs for the weekend, the rules wouldn't allow it, so in my mind, there was a next best option to make sure both my sisters were well taken care of, since the advent of cloning was not a reality. "i know someone who would jump at the opportunity."

"Little bro, I think you know I've got My eye on Jelani." sajira's slick smile made me smile wider. It was like she was reading my mind. "If all goes well, I plan to have him this weekend. he would be the perfect distraction for what has been ailing Me."

"Then we need to make that happen," shamise rebutted. "And I think I know the exact way that we can pull that off, but I'm going to need the both of you to play your parts to make this happen. Sounds like a plan?"

I looked at sajira, giving a knowing wink as she shifted her eyes between the two of us like were about to commit treason. She shook her head as she giggled to herself, realizing that we were about to get into yet more trouble. So, what else was new? "Okay, you two, I'm in. What do You have in mind, sis?"

Chapter Twelve

NEFERTERRI

"my Lady, there are a couple of SUVs here with federal government plates at the front gate, and a Secret Service agent requesting Your presence." Sigma's voice boomed through my earpiece as I was making final preparations for the Marketplace session later. "What is Your ETA, my Lady?"

To say my whole world stopped would be an understatement. I wasn't sure if I wanted to expect this VIP attendee or not, so I kept that information close to the vest in case it didn't come to fruition. While I realized it would be wholly unreasonable to expect her attendance, I held out hope that the promise of complete privacy and the recommendations of several of her colleagues who enjoyed the Thebes compound in northern Virginia would convince her that the trip during her scheduled time away from her Sir and work would be worth it.

Sigma's radio communications in that moment were proof that the efforts were not in vain. "Sigma, please let our guest know I will be there within three minutes."

"Yes, my Lady, relaying the message to the agent now."

I wasn't sure who I wanted to accompany me to the front

entrance to receive this guest, but I decided it was best to maintain a measure of decorum and deal with her myself. It wasn't like we hadn't had high-powered clientele before, but reaching this high was rare air to say the least. Beloved had been communicating with her Sir for some time now, back when he was a US Senator, but with his recent promotion, it had become difficult for him to get out without triggering media frenzies.

My game plan was to have one of his girls to attend the event, and I acquiesced to the presence of Secret Service agents on the premises also. What that meant was for me to explain on the fly to the rest of the attendees that everything was fine, the agents were not looking for anyone, but they were there to protect their assigned official. Considering this was both a one-shot chance for her to cut loose and a rare chance to expand the quality of the clientele a bit, I couldn't leave anything to chance by someone getting a bit star-struck and start running their mouth on social media.

I took one of the golf carts and made my way to the front entrance, where Sigma was waiting for me. His facial expressions had me wondering if he'd been around this type of government appearance before. He didn't give me any indications that he was nervous or anything of the sort. He helped me out of the cart, offering his forearm for me to hold on to while we walked toward the SUVs.

"Did the agent give an idea of who they have with them?"

"No, my Lady, they stated that their orders were to wait until You arrived, and they would allow You to speak to them directly."

I wasn't sure how to receive that information. "That's fine, Sigma, I assume they are in the rear SUV?"

"That is correct, my Lady. I was told once You arrived to escort You to that vehicle and to seat You inside to speak further."

"Are you comfortable with that plan of action, Sigma?"

"No, my Lady, but these are Secret Service agents, and they are acting under orders. In that vein, i am willing to offer a little faith that this is standard operating procedure." Sigma held my arm tight, trying to not sound too protective, but he understood that, Secret Service or not, his directive with regard to my safety overrode everything else.

"Then, let's play it their way for now, and if anything is off-key, I'll make sure to let you know. There was a reason I wanted you by My side for the weekend, and I'm comfortable handling this knowing you know what to do if things go left," I replied as we made it to the rear passenger door of the SUV.

Sigma opened the door for me, ensuring I was comfortable once I was inside, doing his best to avoid staring at the beautiful woman sitting in the seat next to me. He paused for a second, gathering his thoughts before he refocused his attention on me. "i will be outside the vehicle awaiting Your return, my Lady."

Once he closed the door, I turned my attention to the striking beauty sitting in the captain's chair next to me. She nodded toward her agents, who exited the vehicle so we could have some privacy. "Mrs. Alexander, I would like to thank You for making accommodations for Me and My team on such short notice. It is difficult to plan these things out, as I'm sure You can imagine."

"Ms. McAvoy, I am glad that the schedules and stars aligned for You to make an appearance and enjoy Yourself. I'm hopeful that we will be able to provide the type of environment that Your Sir will be comfortable allowing You to indulge in moving forward."

Lea McAvoy was the current White House Press Secretary, so having her in house was a major coup. She didn't get a lot of down time, so the fact that she wanted to spend it at NEBU was a source of pride for me. Coordinating efforts with her Secret Service detail was exhaustive, but in order to have what I wanted, I had to put up with things I might have been uncomfortable with.

Watching her smile was worth every bit of stress I went through. "My Sir is looking forward to hearing about my excursion to Your compound. If everything goes according to plan, He and My sis may require the ability to have You and Yours secure a contingent of Your closest friends and extended family to join us for an event at our private residence out in California at a date to be secured later."

"I'm looking forward to providing You with that experience. Beloved and I are hopeful that Your Sir is able to become the second black POTUS this next election cycle." I leaned back in the seat, doing my best to soak in the gravity of her last statement. In a recent history of game-changing moments, this was the next in a long line of them. "Do I need to make any special accommodations for You and Your detail? All other arrangements have been made to Your specifications."

"My Lady, You have been more than gracious, and that alone is enough for Me to make the call back to DC to speak to My Sir further. I'm sure He, You and Your Beloved will have a lot to discuss moving forward. I can't wait to put Him in contact with You both."

"I'm pleased to hear that, Ms. McAvoy. I'm very certain

Ramesses will be anxious to discuss some next level discretionary measures to ensure that He can balance things out. If His path comes to fruition, those measures will become critical."

I did my best to keep my elation under wraps, but it was difficult to do so in front of her. We'd had a chance meeting at a fundraiser for Vice President Terrell Warren—he was Senator Warren during that time—and once he and Ramesses were in close proximity of each other, the whole "game recognizes game" familiarity drew them together. The ensuing conversation inside the presidential suite at his hotel was still being talked about by amani and the girls, especially when they were able to sit and enjoy it with the Second Lady, Kianna Warren, and Ms. McAvoy.

From that moment forward, we'd been able to maintain streamlined communications with the Second Family, maintaining a heightened level of discretion, to the point to where the only persons who even knew of our connection to them were sworn to secrecy, under penalty of ostracization. We couldn't risk not having access to the circles that they were in, especially if we wanted to implement other phases of the grander scheme with regard to having more exclusive clientele visiting the compounds on a regular basis.

"We can stop with the formalities, Neferterri. You can call Me Lea, and My Sir isn't thinking about the Oval Office yet. There's too much he and President Yeager have to deal with at current, including the current Stateside issues and trying to fund the infrastructure upgrades and other projects to continue to stimulate the economy." Lea shook her head as she realized she was bringing work with her yet again. "Forgive Me, it seems I need this a lot more than I'd originally thought. I didn't mean to bore You with the droning going on inside the District."

"I wouldn't worry about it, Lea, we know it can get to be a bit redundant at times, but we have confidence they will get everything taken care of before the midterm elections come around." I patted her hand to bring her down a few notches so she didn't feel so agitated. "What can I personally take care of for You?"

"Right at this moment, I just want to rest for a bit before the festivities begin later tonight," Lea smiled as she perused the itinerary I'd sent to her on her smartphone. "I'm quite looking forward to the spectacle of this Marketplace session. I doubt I will partake personally in the selection process, but it will be fun to watch it all unfold. The submissive that You screened and vetted for Me will be quite enough for Me to enjoy this weekend. I thank You for that, and that will be enough to recharge the batteries and get back to My Sir and sis."

"Well, please know that if You do have anything, Sigma is the quickest way to get to Me. he is the security director for the event this weekend, and he is in service to Me also," I replied. "Let's get You set up so You can get comfortable, and if You don't mind, I would like for You to get reacquainted with our girls and boy. I'm sure with the bubble that You have to live in up in the District, having some people who aren't in the grinder would be a refreshing respite."

"I'm looking forward to that meeting, My Lady. They were an absolute pleasure to be around, and it helped My sis a lot with being comfortable in her surrender watching shamise and sajira in their interactions around the two of You." Lea leaned toward me, close enough that I could inhale her mango-fresh scent. Her eyes spoke volumes, but I did my best to keep things on the level…for now. "Is there anything that I need to do to make things less distracting for You during Your event? We did our best to be as low-key in our arrival as possible, we don't want to provide any more of a distraction than necessary."

"All I want You to do is unwind, enjoy the weekend, and if You need to have any of the submissives that I have designated to take care of any of Your needs, please let Me know. You have to get back into the fight after this weekend is over, I want to ensure that You have built up enough capacity to deal with the madness." I patted her hand, returning her mischievous grin with one of my own. "We need to do whatever it takes to get You back in the fight and looking *damn* good while doing it. Whatever You need, I got You."

Chapter Thirteen

SAJIRA

This was going to be an interesting evening on levels I wasn't sure I was prepared for. If I was honest with myself, I would have asked Daddy if I could have gone with him to Brazil to help scout the locale for his newest endeavor instead of being here for this weekend. I didn't mind helping with this weekend, but I felt a bit out of place and it was messing with my psyche.

The thing that took me out of my headspace more than anything else was having to assume Top space for the entire weekend. If it was a few hours, fine, but I'd been so accustomed to aligning my will with that of Daddy and Goddess for so long that being out of that space felt foreign, almost like I was betraying them. I felt like those aggressive feelings of wanting to manhandle someone else had been erased from my essence, leaving the woman I was now, the one who reveled in her submissive nature. It was in that space that I felt my most feminine, my sexiest. To set that aside to switch to the other side of the slash—maybe my sis could do it, but I was having trouble reconciling it.

Goddess had a long talk with us about a week before the

event was set to begin, and she made it clear that if either of us began to feel like we needed a "reset" of sorts, that she would be there to handle that. I wasn't a full day into the event, and I was already at the point to where I needed to be controlled as much as I was expected to assume control over the man of my choosing. Tonight's festivities would have us in the great room for the Marketplace session, where the male submissives would present themselves for acquisition by silent auction for the rest of the weekend. I hadn't thought too much about this particular portion of the program, but now that it was happening, anxiety threatened to take over.

I had to consider my options as things played themselves out. My ex-husband would be there, and while my emotions were in check when it came to dealing with him now, my primal instincts were another issue altogether. I had to find a way to avoid those urges coming into play while taking the stroll through the Marketplace. It was almost a given that he would try something to get my attention, but I didn't want him in my space under any circumstances. After his stunt earlier today, I couldn't trust that he would behave by any stretch of the imagination.

The other thing I had to figure out was what I would do once amani was in my personal space. It was no secret that my sis and I had gotten to the point to where we were willing to share everything, and he would be no different in this type of scenario. However, Goddess made it clear that there was enough property to be had, and once we got a look at the men that Hera provided outside of her property, it served to take things to a different level of wild. Still, if I had my choice between amani and the rest of the pieces on display, I'd take amani in a heartbeat, although Jelani presented some very delectable possibilities.

I found shamise among the crowd as Goddess was about to make the announcement that the selection process would begin. I kissed her cheek, smiling when our eyes met. "Are You ready for this?"

"Not really, I'm really nervous and excited, though." She took my hand, patting the back of my palm when she realized I was trembling. "Don't worry, sis, we both know these boys are gonna be so hard up for attention that they might practically jump at the chance of being with any one of us. The bids are liable to be fast and furious."

"I know, but My mind is swirling, I can't think straight." I felt like the room was spinning. I was a fish out of water, out of my element, and it showed. "What am I doing here? I'd rather be in Brazil tending to Daddy instead of being in a space that's been damn near engineered from My psyche."

"That's You trying to fight to be on the other side of the slash, sis, it will pass the minute You win the bid on the one You want. Just enjoy Yourself and get some frustrations out of Your system. It actually might do You some good to balance out a bit." She kissed my lips, quieting any further questions for the moment. "Now, let's wait for Goddess to open the festivities and we can go from there."

We heard the familiar tapping of metal against glass as Goddess asked for quiet without saying a word. God, I swear she makes me moist every time she commands a room. "Ladies, thank You all for your promptness, we wanted to get the boys in place and not have You waiting too long. The rules, of course, are pretty simple: You are not to place a bid on Your own property for the weekend, Your property will only be allowed to contact with You in the event of distress or explicit protocol violation. Each property will have their list of hard limits on their person for You to peruse, along with their kinks and fetishes. Anyone reported for violating protocol will answer to the NEBU Council, as we are the overruling entity at on the grounds. Winning bids will be disclosed discreetly, based on pre-arranged amounts which were purchased as part of Your packages, and the property will be told where they are to report and who they will be in service to. Enjoy, and indulge."

Of course, the minute we were left to our devices, it was on from there! When I say women acted like it was a free for all during a Black Friday sale, that was what was playing out in front of me. shamise kept me close to her, making sure I didn't get caught up in the mix. For all the decorum, it was wild watching the entire scene. The bids were flying all over the map, even though it was a silent auction.

"Holy shit, sis, I don't think Goddess had this in mind when we were talking about this part of the weekend," she remarked as we continued to observe the other Dominas and Tops "inspecting" the merchandise in every way possible. "Have You gotten a chance to see what amani wore for this thing?"

A sly smirk stretched across my face. "I was the one who helped him pick it out and model it for Me after he shipped it to his condo. Whoever wins the bid for him will be in for it tonight."

"I'm planning on that being Me." She grinned as she watched my feigned shock over her brashness. "What, sis? There's nothing in the rules that says I can't have him. After all, we don't own him, Goddess and Daddy do."

I caught the glance from someone I didn't expect to connect with, causing me to ignore a lot of what shamise said. I placed my hand against her chest as I did my best to break the eye contact, but in that moment, I knew who I wanted to bid on. "That's fine, amani will definitely enjoy whatever You have in mind, sis."

Her eyes followed mine, zeroing in on the object of my lust and distraction. "Oh, yeah, that will work and then some. You need to see about that as soon as fucking possible before someone else tries him."

It took me a few seconds for the idea to register in my head. I'd never had a problem going to get what I wanted, but for some reason, apprehension kept me frozen in place. Despite my hesitation, my eyes wouldn't leave from where he kneeled. All I could think about was making him consume every drop of my essence, and there was nothing that would keep me from it, except being in my own head.

"Stop thinking about it and do it, sajira. You know Goddess would say the same thing if She was here." shamise nudged me in his direction, keeping her eyes affixed to her own potential acquisition. "Besides, the sooner You can get what You want, the sooner I can get what I want. Now, chop-chop."

I laughed as she continued to usher me forward, the anticipation making me nervous and excited as we got closer. I frowned when I saw someone beginning her inspection, almost taking an overprotective stance for no reason whatsoever. I wanted what I wanted, and there was no way I wasn't about to allow him to escape me. "Okay, okay, sis, damn. I'm going, I'm going."

"Then hurry up, sis. These women ain't playing tonight."

Before we could get to my destination, someone else managed to tug at my wrap skirt. "Good evening, Ma'am, would You be interested in a trained slave to serve You for the rest of this weekend?"

I looked down, doing my best to turn the sour look on my face off before it betrayed me. This was the last thing I needed tonight. "What do you want, lynx? I don't have time to play games with you tonight."

"Please, Ma'am, i mean no disrespect, but i wanted to present myself for Your approval, with the hope that You will find me suitable for acquisition." He was laying it on thick with the protocol and speech, sounding like he'd been trained well. I was still confused over why he had to have my attention. "It would be my pleasure to serve You in any way You see fit, Ma'am."

"That's not going to happen, and you know the reason why that will never happen." I did my best to control my anger, but I was about to fail in that endeavor. "Touch Me again and I'll have you removed from the compound for violation of the rules."

His look changed the minute the threat left my lips, and all protocol flew out the window. "Oh, so that's how it is, huh?"

"Yes, that's how it always will be, now, make sure that you don't even breathe in My direction or it will get real." I snatched my fabric from his grasp and made my way toward who I wanted the entire time, armed with a heat that needed to be sated with all due haste.

Jelani was still in his kneeling position, patient in his space as he kept his eyes down. I could tell amani helped with his posture and body mechanics, and it only served to ignore my own decorum and take what I believed was mine. "Good evening, Jelani, you may speak with Me now."

Jelani raised his eyes, staring up at me with an intensity that made me weak. "Good evening, my Lady. If i am permitted to say so, You look absolutely beautiful tonight."

If he kept this up, I wouldn't care about all the stares in my direction as I monopolized his time. "Thank you, Jelani, that is sweet of you to say. Have you been enjoying the process so far?"

"No, Ma'am, i can't say i have enjoyed this process, to be honest. Not knowing who has bid on me has been a bit nerve-wracking." His candor was refreshing; I wasn't sure I could have subjected myself to something like this. "But it has been fun in some aspects. i get the chance to talk to You. Forgive me if i'm being a bit forward, but i wanted to say i have a crush on You."

I blushed, itching to make the situation permanent for the weekend. "Would you like for Me to claim you for the weekend, Jelani?"

"Yes, Ma'am, please? It would be an honor to be at Your service for the rest of the weekend."

I saw Mistress Blaze out of the corner of my eye, and from the disgusted look on her face, it was safe to say she wasn't happy with the rules she agreed to. With the mood I was in, there was no way I gave much of a damn what she thought. I did my best to mimic Goddess as I kept my tone as authoritative as possible. "I will ensure that you are Mine this weekend, pretty boy. I'll be placing My bid for you as soon as I leave you. Be ready."

Jelani's body shook the moment I touched his shoulder to leave, all but ensuring that I placed the bid that will keep everyone else at bay and let them know he's off limits and above their pay grade. The only thing that would be left would be to head to my cottage, with every intention of having him do every unspeakable thing I'd been dreaming of him doing to me. Watching the other Dominas and Tops whispering in amazement over what I'd done was a source of pride for me, as I thought it was nothing more than bringing pride to my House, above all else.

"You think You're slick, don't You? You better make sure that You take care of My property while You have him." Mistress Blaze stepped into my path near the doorway leading out the main building.

I couldn't understand why she was being so hostile, but her body language spelled nothing but bad intentions. She acted like I stole her favorite pair of diamonds or something. "I'm sorry, Mistress, I'm trying to get an idea of where all of this is coming from? Is there something I did that has offended You in some way?"

"Honestly speaking, it's Your Goddess who has Me offended, but I guess I have Myself to blame for subjecting My property to something like this."

"Then I'd suggest talking to Your Sis and take it up with Her." I didn't know why it felt so good to return the aggression, but I guessed because I wasn't in my submissive headspace to where I needed to show some reverence, there was no need for me to take whatever she was trying to dish out.

"Don't get used to being on this side of the slash. It isn't as peaches and cream over here, little girl." She insisted on keeping up the pretense that I wouldn't get back with her on all this hostility, so I had to show her that I wasn't the one to play with.

I stepped into her personal space, close enough for her to feel the heat on my skin. I narrowed my eyes and allowed a sneer to spread across my lips. Mistress Blaze stepped back a few paces, only to watch me step forward a few paces to close the distance again. "Oh, no, You don't get to throw darts and not expect to see daggers coming back at You. You plan on giving it, You better be ready to get it. If not, then I'd make another suggestion: call Me a little girl again because You *think* You know who You're dealing with, and I'll make sure You find out just how grown I am. Are we clear?"

"I really don't like Your tone, sajira."

"Are...we...clear...*Ma'am*?" I repeated, waiting for my answer again. "Consider this My last time asking the question."

She continued to look into my eyes, realizing that I wasn't backing down an inch from my stance. In the next moment, she stepped away from me and headed out of the area, leaving me to wonder what was on her mind. If anything, I had a feeling it wouldn't be the last time I would be dealing with her, as long as I had control of her property. I could appreciate her position, and I didn't envy it in the slightest, but what she was not going to do was give me any grief over it.

I put it out of my mind as I headed back to my cottage to prepare for my temporary property's arrival. I had plans, and I was going to make sure he executed them before I had to return him back to his owner.

Chapter Fourteen

NEFERTERRI

"Neferterri, I need to have a word with You."

I was already in defense mode when Blaze came at me with all the hostility of a Comcast customer wanting to cancel their subscription. The energy aura she was giving off felt toxic, almost poisonous to be around, and I wasn't sure if engaging with her in that would have me drained. I couldn't afford to have that happen, but I wasn't about to look like I was avoiding her, either.

"Yeah, Sis, what can I do for You? Are You enjoying Yourself? Have You been able to secure a bid for Your desired bottom? I noticed it has been pretty hyper out there tonight." I figured maybe if I focused on the event that it might put her in a better mood. From the look on her face, I couldn't have been more wrong.

"I'm not enjoying Myself at all, and I'm convinced that there has been some collusion to keep Me from winning the bid for the bottoms I have been interested in." Blaze's eyes were wide and wild, something I wasn't prepared to deal with. Her accusation felt like a kick to the gut, too. "I've lost out on two bottoms of choice, and I'm trying to understand how that was possible when the bids are stacked."

"What would give You that idea?"

"Because Your girls have won the bids on them. Did You rig the session so they would be taken care of?"

I did my best to try to understand why Blaze would levy such a serious charge against me. I hadn't had a chance to even talk to my girls before the event, and amani had been handling things for the VIP clientele, with the exception of me arranging for him to service sajira after the incident with lynx. I took myself out of the registration phase of the event so I wouldn't be seen holding the proverbial fingers on the scale to let those who were closer to me purchase the money for the bidding war during the session. She was aware of all of this; she was there when I agreed to the provision.

That made her accusation even more surprising. "What is going on with You, Sis? You've been giving Me the side-eye whenever we aren't in close proximity, and now that we've had the chance to talk or catch up, You come at Me with this?"

"There's nothing going on with Me, Sis, I'm just trying to find out whether or not You had a hand in Your girls getting what they wanted or not." Blaze seemed to be dead set on getting a yes or no answer on the subject, and she wasn't going to let it rest. "It wouldn't be the first time that You'd gotten what You wanted, so I wouldn't be surprised if You paid it forward…to other people."

"I'm really trying not to feel like You've got some animosity toward Me and I have no idea why You're feeling that way. Have I done something that we need to speak about?" The iciness in her stare was so foreign to me that I had trouble reconciling it. "You've never been so hostile toward Me, and I'm struggling to understand."

"There's nothing for You to understand, Neferterri. Either You helped Your girls get their primary objects of servitude or You didn't. It's not that hard to answer the question, unless You don't *want* to answer the question."

"Look, Blaze, I haven't done a goddamned thing to help My girls. They are more than capable and resourceful to handle things on their own, they always have been." I returned the hostility with some of my own. I might have been a bit in the dark over what the hell she was thinking, but I'd be damned if she was going to steamroll over me like our friendship didn't mean anything. "I resent the implication that I tipped the scales in *anyone's* favor, much less My girls, and I'm irritated that You're making the accusation when *You know Me*."

"I thought I knew You. You've had My back in the past, but the past year or so, I don't know anymore." Blaze shook her head as she scrolled through the recesses of her mind. "I have some things to think about this weekend, and hopefully by the end of this event, we will be able to sit down and have a frank conversation. Until then, I think it's best that we do what we do among ourselves for the duration of the event."

I wasn't in the mood for passive-aggressive nonsense anymore. If space was what she wanted, I could accommodate that and then some. "Whatever works for You, Sis. I still love You, but You're on some next-level craziness right now. I hope You enjoy the weekend in whatever capacity is available to You."

Blaze walked away without another word, leaving me in a confused state of mind. I hadn't done anything that I was aware of, and I did my best to stay off the radar when it came to this event. I was proud of what had been accomplished, but it seemed a bit bittersweet. I didn't keep a lot of women in my circles, and I considered Blaze damn near family. All I could hope for was that she would cool down and we could have an adult conversation.

I deserved that much.

Chapter Fifteen

AMANI

I wanted to pretend that this wasn't a meat market session instead of something that might have felt a little less than that. A lot of the "inspections" going on throughout this portion of the program had nothing to do with where my headspace was regarding this entire situation. I was going to have to get out of my feelings if I was going to get through this in one piece.

I wasn't naïve to what this was supposed to be about, but that didn't mean I had to offer myself up to anyone who felt that I was attractive enough to use me in any way possible, either. Yes, I took pride in the way I presented my body; I'd even managed to get Sir to turn into the proverbial "gym rat" and put himself together quite well, which only benefited the women in our lives. These other dudes didn't hold a candle to me, and I had no problems letting my ego shine with that assessment, even though tiger and Jelani would have begged to differ.

Still, the utter desperation in the voices I heard around me as Domina after Domina continued to peruse among them to figure out which one would be best suited for their needs over the weekend. I looked over at the group of submissives that came in with Mistress Hera and it was all I could do to keep from laughing, but I had to check my privilege, too. Out of the dozen that were over there, only three of them were owned by her.

The rest smacked of desperation.

"Yes, my Lady, i would be honored to offer myself to You and be in service to You this weekend, if it pleases You."

"Ma'am, i can be everything You need me to be. Whatever You desire, it is my will to fulfill."

"Ma'am, nothing would please me more than to make sure You leave this weekend with the biggest smile on Your face."

I listened to all of the madness swirling around me and thought I'd want to vomit. Most of these dudes couldn't spell the word service, much less embody what it meant. If they were really honest, they would tell the Domina interested in them that all they want to do was find a way to get beat and pegged all weekend and leave it at that.

God, I was starting to sound like Goddess. I needed to remember that this was a fantasy bottoming experience, not true acquisition. It wasn't like these were meant to be long-term commitments or anything like that, but I pondered if I should have gone with my first thought and surrendered myself to full-time service to the VIP guests for the rest of the weekend.

I stayed in my kneeling position, waiting for the different Dominas to give me the once over while in my space, preparing for the litany of questions that would soon come after they'd finished eye-fucking me. tiger was next to me, close enough to be within earshot of the thoughts that I didn't realize were sounding out of me.

He did a quick check to see if any of the monitors were

looking before he nudged me. "How much you wanna bet we'll be the last ones standing? These Tops don't wanna catch either of our Owners' wrath if something goes down that we don't want, and the Dominas are busy trying to pick from the slut puppies to get their rocks off."

I chuckled to myself, trying to avoid too much body movement as yet another Domina took a look at me, appreciated the view, and then moved on to the next one. "It is what it is, tiger. To be real, it wouldn't be bad to go back to serving the VIPs, for real. At least they appreciate the nonsexual service that was provided to them."

"Yeah, i'm with you, bro. Mistress was gushing earlier when She found out about how i handled the judge earlier this afternoon." tiger was grinning so much I thought he was trying to sell me a used car or something. "Oh, and word on the street is that Lady Hatshepsut is absolutely enthralled with you, kid. your Goddess is liable to be beaming right now. Proper handling of an Elder is practically a golden ticket."

I hadn't been around long enough to know what that meant, but as long as Goddess was happy with it, that was all that mattered to me. I had no designs on belonging to anyone else, so there was really no agenda to worry about. "i hadn't had the chance to talk to Goddess yet, but She has been busy trying to keep this all together."

"Look, your Goddess adores you and your sisters, there is no doubt in my mind about that," tiger uttered, still keeping an eye out for the monitors to keep from having to deal with that nonsense. "i am worried about your boy, Jelani, though. Mistress Blaze still hasn't locked that down? Something doesn't smell right."

"J will be fine, there is nothing to worry about." If I could have lied any further, I would have combusted on the spot. "What you need to be worrying about is your bro, lynx, losing his mind trying to get my sis to be his Top for the weekend. What was on his mind?"

tiger shrugged his shoulders. "Let's face it, he's not built for this. Dude jumped down the rabbit hole with his wife and it's caused nothing but pain and misery ever since. Maybe he's more of a masochist than we thought. Shit, i'd pay the price of admission to watch him get fucked up by someone who doesn't give a fuck."

Mistress Blaze walked up to us, her eyes locked on me the entire time. I was nervous over how she studied me, feeling a bit self-conscious for the first time all night. Blaze had been staring at me most of the past couple days, to the point to where I wondered whether she had a problem with me or worse—that she had designs on having me this weekend. Her fingers grazed my skin, causing a shiver down my spine. Everything in me told me something wasn't right, her aura was screaming for me to stay away, but I couldn't understand why that was the case.

"Hello, amani, how are you doing this evening?"

"Good evening, Mistress Blaze, how are You this evening?"

"I'm doing well, but I will be doing much better if I could find a submissive to entertain Me for the weekend, and I think I've found him." Blaze's lips curled into a smile that froze me in place. I felt like there was a tinge of malice behind those words. "Don't you want to entertain Me for the weekend, pretty boy?"

To say I was stuck between a rock and a hard place was an understatement. "Ma'am, i…that is to say, well—"

"What he is trying to say, Ma'am, is that he has already been claimed, by winning bid," shamise replied. She walked into the area like she was in on the conversation from the beginning. "I asked him to wait for Me until I was done with handling some business with My sis to get Her squared away. Forgive Me for his not explaining himself, I don't believe he had been told yet that he had been won."

Blaze was confused, and he wasn't the only one. tiger clutched his proverbial pearls on his neck and asked the million-dollar question. "What in the name of Muva is going on here? Did You roll through while i wasn't looking, *Ma'am*? When was the winning bid placed?"

To say it was hard for tiger to call shamise "Ma'am" didn't do his effort any justice. They'd been friends for so long that it was second nature for him to call her "girlfriend" or some other pet name he'd had in mind. I wanted to laugh, but I didn't want Mistress Blaze believing that the fix was in. I wouldn't have cared if it was or not, I didn't want to be claimed by Mistress Blaze. The look in her eyes had three words screaming in my ears: protect the property.

shamise didn't flinch, taking advantage of tiger's penchant to be distracted at a moment's notice. "Yes, as a matter of fact, I did, while you were engaged with another Domina, I made sure everything was settled between Me and amani. The bids have been closing pretty fast on a lot of the properties in here."

Mistress Blaze's body language gave herself away. She felt like the process had been manipulated, and she was not happy about it. "Do I have to call Lady Neferterri in to validate Your claims? I feel like You are trying to skew the rules when they were clearly established before the session started, Ma'am."

"You're more than welcome to do exactly that, Mistress. In

fact, I have no problems enlisting the help of the auctioneers from the Panthers L/L to validate the winning bid for amani." shamise's demeanor, her poise, it turned me on as I watched her stand her ground. It also made me wonder if she'd had this in her all along. "So, would You like to go to the auctioneer or nah? They have been sworn to be completely impartial, if I recall correctly."

Blaze thought about it for a few seconds, then shot a look at tiger as he gave a slow shake of his head that this wasn't the fight she wanted. Her shoulders slumped, resigning herself to not wanting to waste her time. "Fine…tiger, would you like to offer your service to Me for the weekend?"

tiger closed his eyes and sighed, which was never a good sign whenever he did that. He maintained his discipline, never once looking up in her direction. "Ma'am, it would be my honor to be in service to You this weekend, if You have the winning bid, *of course*. Thank You for requesting for me to be in service, but we have been told we cannot influence the bidding process in any way, so, i wish You luck, Mistress."

Okay, that confirmed it. I was in some bizarro world where tiger didn't take advantage of being considered sloppy seconds with some snarky remark. He watched as she headed toward the bidding area to take a look at the remaining property being bid on, sighing when she began speaking to the auctioneer.

"Why i have to be the sacrificial lamb, i'll never know," he mused, almost resigned to the fact that he already knew his fate. "She's cool and all, but She's giving off desperate vibes, and i refuse to have that rub off on me."

"Maybe someone else has placed the highest bid for you already, bro," I offered, not willing to see him have to take one for the team, so to speak. "Don't sell yourself short, your

Mistress hasn't blocked your avenues."

"Oh, this is true, and i'm not worried about it. If anything, it will work itself out to where i am supposed to be," tiger replied. "Now, go ahead and enjoy yourselves, you know tiger finds a way to land on his feet, one way or another."

Mistress Blaze came back to where we were, the visible anger on her face so palpable that everyone in the area couldn't avoid noticing. She shook her head, trying to compose herself as she turned to shamise to speak. "My apologies, my Lady, I have confirmed Your winning bid for amani. I will take My leave now."

I looked at tiger, returning the confused look he gave me as we had yet to figure out the other loose end to this whole conversation. I drummed up the nerve to ask the question on all our minds. "Mistress, forgive me, but are You collecting the property You've claimed by bid?"

Mistress Blaze didn't bother to turn around. Her shoulders slumped, resigned to her fate at having to have picked from the leftover property from the session. "I've been outbid for him, too. A blind bid from a last-minute VIP buyer who wished to have Her identity concealed in the interests that were, as I was told, "disclosed on a need to know, basis". I've been gifted two of Mistress Hera's ponies for My trouble, such as it is. Good evening."

I was floored. Who was the VIP? I thought we'd met them all when they arrived earlier in the day, but I guessed I was mistaken. "Do you have any idea who would have claimed you, sight unseen?"

"Bruh, i'm as clueless as you are, but this has your Goddess written all over it," tiger shrugged. "i wouldn't worry about me too much in this moment, though. you might want to see about the Top who has claimed you for the weekend. She's been waiting long enough. Make sure you have enough fun for me, while you're at it."

shamise bided her time during our exchange, waiting for her opportunity to grab my attention. Once I disengaged with him, I was taken aback by the sea of stares in our direction. I wanted to shrink and disappear over the excessive attention, but the moment shamise's fingers touched my chin to meet her gaze, everyone faded away. "Are you okay, baby?"

I was still so distracted by all the attention, I didn't know how to answer her question. "i…how do i refer to You this weekend? Do i say my Lady, Ma'am…there are so many thoughts running through my head right now."

She kissed me in the middle of my rambling, shutting me down so quick it wasn't even funny. She took hold of me and I wanted her to control every bit of my being in that moment. I admit, I had a crush on her and sajira, but this was becoming more than I'd prepared for. She was always the boss bitch when it was time to get things done, I found that out during the trip to the island, but this was on a whole other level. And I loved it…not as much as I did with Goddess, but I loved it.

"Shh, baby, I need you to look at Me. For this weekend, my Lady will do fine. I'm still trying to figure this all out, too, but I wanted you out of all the others here. If we could have broken the rules, your sis and I would have shared you."

I blushed, but that faded quick when she mentioned sajira. She wasn't the only one I was concerned about. "my Lady, what about Goddess? i didn't see Her moving around the Marketplace tonight, although i wasn't supposed to check around, but You know me. And what about sajira, is She okay, too?"

"Yes, sweetheart, you know how Goddess is." She held out her hand for me to place my leash so we could leave the great room and head to her cottage house. "She has a way of getting what She wants, no matter who or what it is. As far as our sis is concerned, your frat brother should be taking very good care of Her."

Chapter Sixteen

SAJIRA

I leaned over the balcony outside of my bedroom, indulging in one of my favorite kinks as I watched all of the kinky scenes happening all over the compound. I took this time to get my head together while Jelani followed the instructions I left for him to the letter. Tonight would be epic, if I had anything to do with it, and I needed to release some tension after dealing with my ex-husband earlier.

My instructions for him were clear: be naked and hard, on his knees with a glass of wine in one hand and his shaft in the other. From the way we heard Mistress Blaze gush over his girth, I'd planned to take full advantage for as long as it could last. I needed him naked so I could have easy access to every part of his body, considering what I was wearing underneath the satin robe I wore.

Within minutes, I heard the familiar sound of glass colliding with metal. "Ma'am, Your slut is ready, as You instructed."

I took my time entering into the room, wanting to tease him a bit before we got down to what I wanted to do tonight. As much as I wanted to act like I didn't want to consume every inch of him, the truth was that the moment I saw him stark naked and wanting, I'd forget all protocol and immerse myself in lust and carnal activity. I closed my eyes and exhaled before pulling the blinds back to readjust to the lighting inside the cottage.

Jelani's eyes were all over me, acting like he was as eager to devour me as I was in commanding him to do it. "Ma'am, oh my God, You look absolutely stunning."

I blushed, but I kept my wits about me, reminding myself of the headspace I was supposed to be in. "Thank you, Jelani, now be a good boy and bring Me the wine in your hand."

As he took care to crawl to me to present my wine glass, my body began to betray me quicker than I was prepared for. If I wanted this fantasy to play out, I needed to be more disciplined. In that moment, I understood how hard it must be for Goddess when she's around amani.

He was close enough to resettle into his kneeling position, presenting the glass to me with his head bowed. "Your wine, chilled and for Your enjoyment."

I took the glass from him, staring into his eyes as I pulled on the tie to my robe, exposing my naked form underneath. I watched his eyes take hold of my voluptuous landscape, waiting for the moment he would see the surprise I had waiting for him. I felt desired, wanted, it made me so moist I was worried the piece would slip out of my yoni.

His eyes widened, a smile spreading across his face. He tried to recover, lowering his eyes before I could correct him, doing his best to keep in his kneeling position.

"Is there something that has caught your attention, Jelani?"

"Yes, Ma'am, it has. You're wearing a strap-on and harness, Ma'am."

"And why does that have you grinning like a Cheshire cat?"

"Forgive me, Ma'am, but it is one of my hard-core kinks."

This was getting more interesting by the second. I read the list that was attached to him while we were in the Marketplace, so I knew pegging was something he enjoyed, among other things that I could take advantage of over the course of the weekend. "And have you indulged in your hard-core kink before? Do you like to be pegged?"

A slight frown washed over his face as his shoulders slumped. "Forgive me, Ma'am, but i have not been able to indulge as of yet. i…i'm a virgin when it comes to pegging, but it is one of my deepest fantasies."

"Why haven't you fulfilled it?"

"Vanilla women don't care for it too much. The last one told me she didn't do bisexual men."

"What about Mistress? Why hasn't She taken care of that with you?"

"Mistress has been a bit…well, She has been wanting to focus on my service aspect before She sees fit to open the rest of our relationship up to other things." Jelani's body language shifted, as much as he tried to hide his irritation. "If i have an urge, as long as my tasks have been handled, She allows me to use Mistress Sinsual's nymph to take the edge off."

In that moment, I took off my robe, climbed on top of him and wrapped his legs around my waist. "you belong to Me for the weekend, which means you will fulfill My desires. One of those desires is to peg a male bottom, so, it looks like you get to pop My cherry, and I get to pop yours, and from what I'm feeling pressing against My stomach, you seem very excited to have this happen."

"Yes, Ma'am, very much so, if i'm allowed to say."

I kissed him deeper, no longer in the mood to talk. I reached for the coconut oil, lifting up long enough to drip small dollops around his shaft and balls, letting it coat his skin. "Stroke him for Me, slut. Get him nice and hard for Me."

He did as he was told, his moans turning me on and fueling my aggression as I took the dildo and coated it with the oil, getting it as slick as I could before I placed the condom over it. I slipped a finger over his perineum, teasing around his anal cavity, feeling him flinch a bit when I got close to sliding my coated finger inside him.

"Oh fuck!" He cried out, still stroking as he focused his attention on my breasts.

I slipped a finger in, feeling him shudder underneath me. The rush was more intense than I'd ever imagined as I pushed deeper. "Mmmm, it sounds like I found someone's G-spot. Do you like the way that feels, baby?"

"Yes, Ma'am, it feels incredible. Please, don't stop, please!" His thighs tightened, eyes closing tight as his body gave himself away in an instant. "Ma'am, i'm gonna...shit, i'm—"

"Not yet, baby, not yet." I removed my finger and placed my other hand over his to calm him. He looked so cute as he pouted and gyrated his hips, a silent plea to push him over the edge again. "I promise I'll let you come soon enough, understood?"

He nodded as I moved him into the position I wanted him in. I kissed him once more, looking into his eyes to make sure I had his attention. "Tell Me what you want, slut."

"Fuck my ass, Ma'am."

"Say it again."

"Please, fuck my ass, Ma'am. Fuck Your slut."

I moved my phallus up and down his opening, pausing to tease and push part way in, allowing the head of the shaft to slip inside. I continued to drip the oil over the opening to keep it slick as I pushed further inside, feeling his muscular thighs wrap around my waist again, pulling me even further inside. "Mmmm, eager little fuck toy, aren't we? Do you want it all the way in? It's pretty big, slut."

He nodded, doing his best to keep his hands off me unless he was directed to do so, still stroking as I began a slow in and out stroke to give him time to open up to me. "Please, Ma'am, give it all to me. It's Yours to take, please take it!"

I buried it to the hilt, feeling my clit rubbing against the base of his shaft and balls. I pulled out halfway, slamming back inside, grinning as I heard him cry out in a pain-pleasure mix that I was all too familiar with. I lost myself in the sensations and sounds as I increased my strokes. "How does it feel, baby?"

"Yes, Ma'am, it hurts so good. Fuck me harder, please, hurt me." Jelani was so far gone that his body met my strokes even when I wasn't stroking inside him. "Oh, fuck, i can't hold back, Ma'am, can i come, please, can i come?"

I grabbed his hips, driving in as deep and fast as I could, wanting to take him over the edge and further with each furious stroke. The constant pounding against my clit was enough to have me drown in my own orgasmic wave soon. "Stroke your dick for Me, slut. Come for Me, give it all to Me!"

Jelani started growling. He sounded so fucking sexy that he triggered my feral urges to scratch and bite him as he erupted. He arched his back as streams of his essence shot toward my chest and stomach. "Oh fuck, Ma'am, fuck i'm coming! i'm coming!"

I squeezed tight against the bulb still lodged against my G-spot, and it was only a matter of time before the surge coursed through me. I pulled out of him, unlatching the harness from my hips as quick as I could, rushing to place my throbbing sex over his face. "Make Me come, slut! Now! Make Me come all over your face!"

His tongue felt like it was attached to an electrical socket, causing shockwaves to race through my body as I felt wave after wave take me deeper into the darkness. I called out to every deity in existence as my climax continued to lay siege to every erogenous zone I had. Before long, I collapsed into a heap next to Jelani, falling into a deep, comatose sleep that I'd hoped I wouldn't wake from until at least midmorning.

Chapter Seventeen

NEFERTERRI

The thing about being the programming director of an event that sucked the most was that there was never enough time in the day to be able to handle everything and still get what I wanted and needed at the same time. I had to ensure everything went off without any incidents last night during the Marketplace session, but it came at a cost, as the properties that I would have been in the thick of the bidding process most of the night were already won. I didn't take it as a personal slight of my sex appeal, but it made more and more sense as to why my Beloved always made sure one of the girls was available to him during these events.

I took inventory over the pairings for the rest of the weekend, and I smiled over the fact that both my girls were able to secure the winning bids for the objects of their respective desires. It was also interesting of note that Mistress Blaze won the bid for lynx, Sinsual's other slave, while Mistress Hera won the bid for tiger, while Sinsual won the prize of the night, winning the bid for karimi El, Lady Norene's charge. All in all, it was a successful session, and I was looking forward to a lot of the scenes playing themselves out.

I didn't wallow in my own self-pity, though. Being the programming director still had its benefits, one of those being the security director being at my beck and call on more than a few levels. Sigma and I had developed a connection throughout the evening, and it was noticeable whenever we were around each other. Truth be told, I couldn't wait to have him when the time and opportunity presented itself.

I rose from my bed, intent on easing into my day the best way possible, preparing my mind for the first set of intensives that were scheduled for the noon hour. The moment I left my room, one of the volunteers awaited me.

From the look on his face, it wasn't something he wanted to be the one to bring to my attention. "my Lady, forgive the intrusion, but there is another person at the gate requiring Your approval."

I wanted to find the first wall and throw a sledgehammer into it. It was coming to a point to where I wondered if the underground marketing worked a little too well. We'd closed off any new prospects of attendance weeks ago, but there were still people coming down to gain access.

"Who is this person, and where did they come from? Are they local? Never mind, it doesn't matter, I'm not sure if I want to approve another impromptu guest." I rubbed my hand over my face to figure out how to change my demeanor as we made our way to the golf carts. Sigma awaited our arrival, which put a smile on my face.

"my Lady, the guest has been bound and gagged, and a note has been attached to him to be opened only by You," Sigma explained as we rode to the main entrance. "It's rather unorthodox to see this particular presentation. According to the morning detail, he has been out there for about twenty minutes."

Sigma was right, that was unusual. "I'll make My assessment when we arrive, Sigma. I'm intrigued by the presentation and the fact that whomever left it made sure I was the only one to read the information."

"Permission to inspect the packaging before You approach, my Lady?" Sigma's military background shone through, making me moist over his need to be overprotective. A girl could get used to this. "The last thing i want is for You to be compromised."

"Permission granted, Sigma. I don't believe anyone would want to go to such lengths to try and harm Me, especially with the men I have around Me," I replied. I placed my hand over his to give a gentle squeeze, a silent gesture of my appreciation. "However, we can't be too careful."

"My sentiments exactly, my Lady. Besides, it's my job to ensure You do not encounter too much stress during this weekend and, if needed, be a conduit for any stress relief You wish to engage in." Sigma's arm flexed for a moment, and watching the muscles twitch made something else twitch when I was supposed to be concentrating on the situation at hand.

We arrived at the main entrance and, sure enough, the submissive was hogtied in a prone position, a note attached to his forehead. He was a Caucasian male, and he looked familiar, but I couldn't place my finger on where I recognized him from. Sigma's head cocked to the side, trying to assess what was in front of us. A quick nod from me prompted his approach as he took care in removing the gag from the submissive's mouth.

"Who dropped you off at the NEBU compound?" Sigma's

first question wasted no time in getting to the heart of the matter. "What is the reason you were dropped off here?"

The submissive strained his neck to acknowledge Sigma, but he didn't respond for several minutes. He didn't look happy to be in the predicament he was in at the moment, the embarrassment was written all over his face. "i was instructed by my Mistress to respond to questions after the note attached to my forehead is read. i am not being disrespectful by being silent, as the note will explain my presence here."

Sigma took notice of the envelope taped to his forehead, grabbing a latex glove from his pocket to retrieve it. He took a vial of some sort from his other pocket, unscrewing the dropper and squeezing a couple of drops onto the envelope. After a few seconds, he opened the envelope, placing a few droplets onto the paper in a presumed attempt to make sure there was nothing harmful to me before handing it to me.

He turned to me, dropping to his knees to present the contents of the letter to me. "my Lady, the letter is safe to touch and peruse."

I took the letter from his hands, giving another gentle squeeze to acknowledge his effort, unfolding the paper to figure out who would have gone to such lengths to leave property unattended. As I continued to read the note, all of the curiosity I had was satisfied in a few words.

Lady Neferterri,

> *Please forgive the unorthodox nature of My leaving this pitiful excuse for a submissive at Your event, but I felt the need to have him punished for his behavior. He disappointed Me and placed himself in the public eye with his disrespectful behavior on social media. he is*

to endure whatever depraved and humiliating undertaking that You see fit as a condition of his reentry into My House and service. Failure to comply would be tantamount to permanent release. I trust You will handle him in the manner that I am confident You will see fit.

In Leather,
Mistress Lohyna

I almost choked from surprise when I read who the note was from. Mistress Lohyna was a long-time member of the Houston Leather community before she moved here to Atlanta. She got caught up in a high-profile investigation into her ex-husband's attempted murder of a submissive that Dom and Beloved handled, resulting in her eventual clearance of any wrongdoing by Dom. She's a bit of a free spirit, but her penchant for discipline and punishments were legendary.

Looking down on the poor soul still hogtied on the ground, he must have done something big to warrant the type of near abandonment she proposed in the note. "It seems you've really pissed off your Mistress. What is your name?"

"my Lady, my name is Earl, and i want to apologize for having placed You in the position You are in." He continued to struggle in his binds as he tried to speak loud enough for me to hear him. "It is my hope to subject myself to whatever creative devices You deem fit in order for me to fulfill the requirements of Mistress and gain favor back into Her House."

I looked at Sigma, who did his best to avoid the smirk on his face like he already knew the answer to the questions in my mind. "What's so funny, Sigma? Care to share with the rest of the class?"

"my Lady, at the risk of sounding flippant, but do You know who this jackass is?" He paused for a second while he waited for my confused expression to manifest itself. "This lowlife politician came for Congressman John Lewis on social media about a month ago. To be honest, i'm ready to request to be a part of whatever pain he may need to endure for that transgression alone."

I clamped my hand over my mouth to stifle a scream when I connected the dots. *That's where I know him from!* "Oh, I just might grant that request…among others that I'm going to want you to fulfill for Me."

The security detail didn't want to give themselves awy, but it was easy to tell that they wanted to be a fly on the wall of whatever we had going on. I noticed one of the Pearls start to giggle, but I didn't want to give them anything more than they wanted to use for whatever gossip that would come later in the day. This time, I wanted Sigma to know I was more than interested in working him over in more ways than one.

"my Lady, it would be my pleasure to ensure Your pleasure." Sigma took out a knife to cut the rope binding Earl, allowing his body to unfurl from the tightly coiled position he was in. "Now, as far as this maggot is concerned, what would You like to do with him? i am at Your disposal for whatever You decide to do, my Lady."

His animated enthusiasm was enough to amp me up a few notches, but I had to settle my emotions to get to the next idea in my head. "When the time comes, Sigma, I will make sure you're the first to know. Now, Earl, per Mistress's wishes, I will allow you entry, with a tight leash on you. If you so much as breathe wrong in a Domina's direction, consider your reentry inside Mistress's House revoked. Are we clear?"

"Yes, my Lady, we are clear."

"Good, now get with My coordinator to figure out where your talents can be best served before we figure out what needs to be done to earn your way back into Mistress's good graces." I watched Earl climb to his feet, making sure his eyes never met mine as he was ushered to where he was supposed to go.

Sigma stepped within whispering distance, his cologne tripping my senses fantastic as he mused about our newest "whipping boy". "Do You think the rest of the submissives will cut him any slack?"

I laughed, shaking my head several times. "The minute tiger gets a hold of him, it will be a wrap!"

Chapter Eighteen

AMANI

I wasn't sure what to make of the scene out near the gazebo in the back of the main building, but I had a feeling it was something I needed to be clued in on. We were on a scheduled break from servitude to socialize a bit before things picked back up a little later in the evening. I figured it was a chance to get a lay of the landscape, to get a look at some of the submissives from out of town and perhaps get a feel for them and vice versa.

There was a larger group than usual hanging around the pool area, but I had to admit that it was a welcome sight. It's not often that submissive males were willing to be out and public, and even more rare that submissive males of color were willing to. A lot of the different mix of ethnicities might as well have made this a microcosmic version of the United Nations—including the countries who made you, as my grandma used to say, shake your head and say, "Bless their little hearts".

There was this one guy who, if it weren't for the fact that he was so ashy he looked like he dropped a bag of flour over his body before he came out the cottage this morning, might have been sexy enough to draw a hell of a lot of attention from the men and women alike. Just looking at him required me to go back to shamise's cottage and find the industrial-sized container of coconut oil or something to remove all of that dead skin.

I wasn't the only one who took notice for all the wrong reasons. tiger had his nose turned up so much, I thought he'd detected a pungent scent emanating from him as we began to converge on the larger group.

"Where in the world did Casper the Friendly Ghost come from, amani?"

"i don't know, tiger, but you gotta admit, he's well put together. Do you know who he arrived with?"

"Man, word I've been getting is that he came with that chick who tried you and your Goddess a while back, Lady Norene. That's gotta put some things on pause with regard to even trying to rock with Ashy Madison on a GTK basis."

Despite tiger's constant roasting of ol' boy, hearing her name pressed the pause button, alright. I hadn't heard that name in a little over a year when she challenged Goddess while trying to ogle me on the slick. How on earth she was able to get inside of this event was anybody's guess, but I knew that Goddess wouldn't have allowed it under any circumstances. Something was off. "It's probably best to figure out what this guy's angle is anyway, since he is supposed to be one of us for the weekend."

"Look, bruh, you know there's no pressure to be worrying about the competition," tiger replied. "But, since you wanna see about ol' boy, let's see if the brains match the physique."

We walked over to the group, comprised of the male submissives and slaves who had some down time during the designated rest period that was scheduled so we could decompress from the previous night's events. I saw Jelani and lynx, and a couple of other submissives that I hadn't had the chance to cross paths with, but the center of attention was Lady Norene's submissive, without a doubt.

As we walked toward the group, tiger snapped his fingers like he'd forgotten something to talk about. "Did you get word that there's a couple of politicos around here? i'm still bugging out on the luck i found myself in."

"Nah, bro, not a word, but you know Goddess would have kept that under wraps, and probably anyone else that She would have entrusted to help with that," I replied. To be honest, I had an inkling that one of Vice President Warren's submissives would be the one that might have made it down. She and shamise have the same Alpha temperament, despite surrendering their will to their respective Dominants. "Why, what luck did you find yourself in?"

"The freaking White House Press Secretary was the one behind the blind bid to acquire me for the weekend!" He tried his best to contain his excitement, and I couldn't blame him for wanting to shout to the rooftops. "i almost fainted when i was presented to Her fine ass."

I laughed out loud at that statement. "you better not let Mistress hear you gushing like that. She's liable to kill you for it."

"Mistress is the Alpha and Omega of my universe, but that does not negate the fact that Lea McAvoy is finer than frog's hair, bruh!" He was still fanning himself as he thought about it. "But that wasn't the only snap surprise of the weekend. Remember that politician on the north side of town who tried to come for Congressman John Lewis?"

"Yeah, i remember that dude."

"One of the ProDommes currently has Her hands on him, making him do all kinds of stuff." He shook his head, trying to figure out what else he could divulge. "your Goddess is gonna end up passing him around like a damn rag doll to whomever wants to psychologically fuck him up in the most creative way possible."

"i can't think of anyone better than your Mistress, bro. She'd be liable to have him so screwed up that by the time he leaves NEBU, he won't look at another person of color without being triggered." It was no secret that Mistress Sinsual was a master hypnotherapist, and that was a dangerous thing to be if you pissed her off. The last submissive who needed "readjusting" ended up barking like a dog every time he had the nerve to call a woman a bitch in a negative fashion.

"Look, i will personally request for Ms. McAvoy to request an audience just to watch that happen," tiger said. "That would be one epic story to take back to Her Sir and Congressman Lewis. Sweet justice on all kinds of levels."

I nodded in agreement as we got closer to the group. "i guess we need to be social, so, let's get to it so we can figure out what all the excitement is about."

Within seconds of catching the conversation, it was clear why he'd garnered so much talk time. "i'm not actually a submissive, i'm more of a switch, but i lean more toward my Pharaonic Lord Dominant side."

tiger's head cocked to the side, and I already knew dude was in for it on levels that he wasn't quite ready for. He didn't go off half-cocked just yet; he needed to get a gauge on what was being discussed. "Good afternoon, fellas, all is well, yes?"

Jelani was the first to respond, doing his best to stifle a

chuckle. "What's good, tiger? We were actually sitting here discussing our various Dominas and our relationship to them, and karimi El was telling us that he doesn't belong to Lady Norene, or anyone for that matter. It had some of us curious over why he was here."

tiger nodded, turning to the half-dressed piece of chocolate goodness and narrowed his eyes, studying him for a few moments. The question popped up out of nowhere. "Good afternoon, karimi El, pleased to meet you. i would get the formalities out of the way, but we ain't got time for all that right now, what i want to know is, for those of us who just popped up on the conversation, could you please explain to the cheap seats what in the hell a Pharaonic Lord Dominant side of anything is?"

lynx tried to intercept the conversation before his sub brother could ramp up. "Come on, bro, let's not start up today. Dude said he was a switch, we were trying to get a better understanding of what his headspace was like."

"What we not gon' do right now is try to shush me like you didn't hear that BS that came out of his mouth, bro. It's in your best interest to sit down and listen when grown men are talking." tiger stared lynx into subjugate dismissal, returning his attention to karimi El. "Now that that madness is out of the way, could you please enlighten us on this 'concept' of yours?"

"Well, it's not a concept, it's something that has been around for thousands of years, but i wouldn't expect anyone here to know anything about it." karimi had already begun his counterattack on tiger, but I didn't think he realized what he was getting himself into. "A Pharaonic Lord is a Dominant who expects and thrives on the devotion and worship of his submissives and slaves. It is relatively common for the real-life households of Pharaonic Lord Doms to forsake all traditional forms of religion in order to practice their own home-grown religion, with the Dominant at its head and submissives and slaves as religious acolytes. In such cases, the Dominant is usually regarded by his submissives and slaves as a near-deity, or as a prophet of God."

"Go on, i need the whole kit and caboodle before i say another word, dude," tiger remarked.

"i would prefer that you not address me in such a peasant manner, if you please. While i realize what headspace i am supposed to be in for this event—which Pharaonic Lords are not really supposed to be engaged in, as we prefer more private events—it is in the best decorum to at least use terms that aren't relegated to the streets."

tiger shook like someone had zapped him with an electric cattle prod. He closed his eyes for a few more seconds before he composed himself long enough to speak again. "Continue, please."

"Thank you, i appreciate your ability to comply," karimi paused for a few seconds like he was trying to access the madness in his brain again. "Yes, Pharaonic Lords tend to keep large poly households of at least four or five slaves, depending on how many they can afford to maintain, and those slaves have uniquely defined roles within the dynamic. In the Kemetic tradition, we shed our slave names in order to don the names of our Egyptian descendants. When not around submissives as i am right now, my name is Lord Pharaoh Muwaan Mat."

After a few more moments of listening to this man talk, tiger had had enough. "Okay, first of all, don't confuse this

Pharaonic Lord drivel for the Hotepian nonsense that you are all descendant from the Egyptians when none of you can even name any of the Nubian lands south of Egypt nor understand their significance to the Egyptian empire at the time. Second, your name, if that was what you chose, doesn't even translate from any dialect or language in the African diaspora. It's the name of a Mayan king, and i should know; i teach history when i'm not being the submissive extraordinaire that everyone has come to know and love, you ignorant bastard."

"i will not have you speak to me—"

"Then i suggest that you get to rolling up out of here with the first thing smoking, home boy, or i'll be sure to make you regret your stay here in NEBU." tiger stared karimi El down, daring dude to flex on him and start a fight. "Oh, and for the record, there is an already established Pharaoh, no, scratch that, there are *two*, and they have been for the better part of twenty years—they *earned* the fucking right to be called Pharaoh, not some Hotepian trick regurgitating propaganda to make himself look bigger than he already is."

"i've heard about your established Pharaohs, and while they have been recognized as Pharaonic Lords, they are not a part of the Order of Pharaonic Lords." karimi stood his ground as best he could, but his eyes widened as his anger rose. "We consider them rogue, and their exploits are considered an affront to the Order."

"Oh my God, now i've heard every damn thing." tiger was about at the end of his rope. "So, this *Order* you speak of, do any of the members of this madness even deal with anyone outside of the confined walls of this group masturbation circle? What have they done that is of any merit? Any contributions to the national scene? Any sponsoring of regional conferences?"

"Those conferences and events are beneath Pharaonic Lords, and if we do decide to engage in them, we would rather spearhead the effort, rather than have someone who has not been vetted and screened properly take the point."

The words he spoke might as well have been spoken in another language. Verbiage like that was not something that Sir or Master Amenhotep would have condoned in any form. In fact, one or both would have found the quickest way for this dude to exit, with all due haste. He was getting away with bloody murder with each word out of his mouth.

"i like how you just sat there and said a whole bunch of nothing to justify what we already figured out before you opened your mouth. And for the record, this is a *private* event. you and your sorry excuse for a Domina that you do or don't claim as yours got away with a software glitch, otherwise you wouldn't have stepped foot onto this compound." tiger was on a roll, and there was no way anyone was going to stop him. "you didn't answer my question, but it doesn't matter, you need to be dismissed outright and sent home since you insist on being in this confused headspace."

"you're the one coming at me, attacking something you don't understand, and then you and this gentleman want to flout rogue Pharaohs like they are the gold standard." karimi's tone became more accusatory and condemning by the minute. "As far as i'm concerned, they need to be stripped of their titles immediately, and if the others in the Order were here, they would concur with my sentiment."

"i don't take kindly to you speaking of my Sir, or Master Amenhotep, in the manner of which you are, karimi," I inserted myself in the conversation, not in the mood to hear any more of this mess any longer. "It would be in your best interest to cease any references to my Sir or Master Amenhotep if you know nothing of either of them in any capacity."

karimi blinked a few times when he heard me reference Ramesses, taking a moment to collect himself. "Now i know you did not refer to a Pharaoh, rogue or not, as your Sir? Pharaohs, Pharaonic Lords, are not bisexual, nor do they hold dominion over any male submissives or slaves. It's bad enough this whole fantasy weekend is even taking place, now you wish to subject me to blasphemy on top of that?"

"Where in the bloody hell have you been living, dude? It's 2017, not the goddamned fifties." tiger was three steps shy of breaking him down, and I was ready to drop him where he stood before he could get to this jackass. "This is how this is going to go down, okay? We gon' forget about any of this nonsensical rhetoric you spitting right now, and in exchange for you getting back in your submissive headspace and acting accordingly, we will consider not taking you out in the woods and beating you within an inch of your life. Sound like a winner to you?"

"you wouldn't dare put your hands on me. That is against the rules of the event and, i presume, the compound also." karimi didn't seem too concerned about the way this was turning. "But even if i decided to indulge you, you couldn't take me, not one on one."

"Keep running your mouth about things you know nothing about and i promise you something bad will happen to you, bruh." I wasn't in the mood for his faux controlled temper any longer. I learned what that looked like up close from one of the best in the business, and even he could explode if the circumstances were right. "you are not the baddest man on the block, partner, and you're not in your element. Do us all a favor and stay in your lane, there's no one to get in your way, feel me? your choice, but if i were you, i would choose very carefully."

He looked me up and down, sizing me up for a second, meeting my stare with one of his own. In a surprising move, he backed down. "No pressure from me, man, I wouldn't dream of rocking in hostile territory. For what it's worth, i admire your loyalty to your Dominants. Not many would have challenged, and i respect that. i hope the rest of you enjoy the weekend, i know i will."

He stepped away from the group, leaving everyone confused over what the hell just happened. I shook my head, realizing that he was no different than most of the other Hoteps I'd run into when I lived in New York and DC. All that had to be done was step up and meet them at their bullshit and they shut the fuck up.

"Sooner or later, he's going to have to sit down and humble himself," tiger mused as we took our seats to continue the other sidebar conversations. "One monkey ain't about to stop this show, and it's a helluva show, dammit! Now, let's enjoy this break before we have to get back to business."

Chapter Nineteen

SHAMISE

"Don't you think for a minute that you're getting treated any differently, pretty boy. I'm not Goddess, but I want to make sure this experience is good for both of us."

"Yes, my Lady, i understand. It has been weird having You assume control over me this weekend, i will admit."

"It's been an eye-opening experience for me, too, baby. I think I'm still better off in My primary headspace, but I think I can enjoy doing a little Topping by command."

amani and I were having a conversation in the early evening hours at my cottage, taking some time to indulge as shared property of Kemet-Ka as opposed to Top and bottom. Even though we were having that conversation, we decided it was best to still maintain generic protocol and decorum, which had him at my feet in his place. It was an interesting added aspect to our relationship, one that I believed drew us a bit closer.

In the midst of the conversation, I began to miss sajira. We were so used to having these conversations among the three of us that it felt like something was lacking, to a degree. I enjoyed the fact that she could let her hair down a bit with Jelani, though, and I couldn't wait until they sat down with us in a little while to swap stories and give us a different perspective on how things were going.

"The funny thing, my Lady, is that You've gotten more comfortable than we both thought You would." amani smiled for a moment, thinking about the way I'd been handling him. "You've been around Goddess the longest, so it would be easy to guess that some of Her rubbed off on You."

I hadn't thought about that perspective, and he brought up a good point. I'd been introducing myself as the Alpha slave within the House for so long that I guessed I hadn't paid attention to how much I'd embodied that role. I thought back to all of the preparations we were making while getting the island up and ready to go, and how much Daddy and Goddess had entrusted me with as much as they did. Even with this event prep, it took me by surprise over how much responsibility Goddess had turned over to me.

"you know what, you're right, amani. Maybe Goddess had been a bit more hands-off when it came to what we needed to get done. It freed Her up to handle some other stuff, and I guess that was my primary focus as Her property." I caressed his cheek, watching him smile at the isolated attention lavished on him. "I don't have any intentions of abusing that positioning. If anything, it's the evolution that Goddess and Daddy had always envisioned within the House itself."

"i'm still blown away by the way things have moved and how quickly they've happened in such a short time for me, my Lady." amani was in full-blown muse mode, and I enjoyed the way his mind was processing everything. "When we spoke about expectations in the beginning and where things may end up over time, i honestly didn't envision the things that are happening to us now."

"That's the funniest thing about Daddy and Goddess, baby boy; They are full of surprises, but it only looks like surprises because They're constantly trying to figure out what we can get ourselves into." I laughed at some of the sponsoring we'd done over the past couple years, including some of the things we'd done at NEBU with regard to regional and national conferences, doing our best to help keep Atlanta on the map and on pace with the other cities that host larger conferences, despite being in the Bible Belt. "If anything, there's only going to be more coming down the pipeline, and I'm here for it. It keeps things interesting."

amani laughed, shaking his head over the sheer exhaustion of thinking about the things we as a Leather family get involved in. "There are some days when i wonder if it's too much, but then when we have a day where there's nothing on the calendar, it has me all out of sorts."

"The best thing to do on those days is to find the time to build the capacity and energy you need to prepare for the next event, amani." I didn't want him to believe for a minute that I had this endless abundance of energy reserves. I needed my "me" time, too. "As much as I love this family dynamic, I have to be able to get things back into balance so I can be what They need."

A knock on the door interrupted our mini vibe session. I directed amani to receive the unexpected guests, getting myself comfortable while switching my headspace back into the left side of the slash. I wasn't quite done with our talk, but I resolved to pick it back up the minute we're able.

Imagine our pleasant surprise at who was on the other side of the door. The smile on amani's face was all the confirmation I needed, and it was needed on so many levels that it wasn't even funny. "Oh my God, we didn't expect to see any of you until later in the day."

Goddess's glow was evident as she stepped through the door with sajira and Jelani in tow. The boys made sure we were comfortable as we took our seats, taking their respective places at our feet. I realized we were supposed to be in Top space, but I couldn't resist wanting to rest at Goddess's feet, if only for a moment of balance. I noticed the same thing was happening with my sis, but we did our best to resist those urges in front of the boys.

Questions were abounded to say the least, and amani made sure to get my permission before he unleashed the flood. "Goddess, how are You holding up over this weekend? What have You been doing this whole time? Have You had someone to serve You for the weekend?"

Goddess couldn't stop laughing, but she knew we would be concerned about whether she was burning herself out trying to make sure this weekend went off without any incidents. "Yes, baby boy, I am doing okay, things have been going very well this weekend and I am happy about that. I haven't had the time to really indulge in anything in particular just yet, but Sigma has made himself available to Me, at My whim."

I looked at sajira, and we fanned ourselves at the same time. Sigma was about as prime choice of a specimen as anyone could get, but since he wasn't on the menu during the Marketplace session, no one thought to consider him as a viable option. I guess it's good to be Goddess after all.

Jelani was a bit quiet throughout the impromptu chat, content to being stroked like a satisfied pet while at sajira's feet. In fact, he looked a bit too content. "you're looking like you're happy My sis claimed you, Jelani. Have you been taking good care of Her?"

Jelani blushed, looking up at the glow on sajira's face before he dropped his head to avoid eye contact with me. Goddess grinned as she took notice of his facial expressions, too, focusing her attention on him. "I think that explains everything we need to know. your Mistress will be pleased to hear you are handling yourself well."

In the next instant, Jelani's expression went from jovial to pensive. If the room could have dropped a few degrees, despite the Georgia heat, it would have felt like we were in the middle of December. "Thank you, my Lady, but if i could make the request that She not be told. i realize i might be violating protocol for the weekend, but She has no ties to me at this point."

To say the confused looks on our faces was an understatement. I looked at amani, and all he could do was shake his head like he'd already been privy to what his frat was going to say. I watched sajira continue to console him, almost in a protective manner, which threw me off even more. "Okay, what exactly is going on with you and Mistress, Jelani? Whatever it is, it is kept in confidence here."

Jelani hesitated for a moment, looking to sajira for guidance. sajira, in turn, looked to Goddess for guidance, leaving Goddess to be the final word on the matter. Goddess gave a silent nod, causing sajira to tap Jelani's shoulder in a comforting manner, giving him the opening to speak in a safe environment. "my Lady, She has been, well, it's hard to explain."

"Do your best, Jelani. If there is anything I can do to help, I will try." Goddess laid back in her chair, getting comfortable as we waited for the story to unfold.

Jelani took a breath and exhaled. "Mistress was great in the beginning, but then about a month ago, She seemed to be focused on something else. Whatever She wanted me to do, i made sure it was handled, but She seemed like it wasn't enough. After a while, i just rolled with it, it wasn't fun for me anymore."

Goddess closed her eyes, nodding for a moment like she might have had a clue about what was going on. "I'll make sure to talk to Mistress when I get the chance. She's been a bit scattered and distracted, even here this weekend. I need to make sure She's okay."

I wasn't so sure about what was going on with Mistress Blaze, but some of the events of the previous night began to make sense. "Goddess, Mistress was a bit more than distracted during the Marketplace session. If anything, I could have sworn She was pissed off when I claimed amani, like She had an agenda that got blown out of the water the minute he was claimed."

Goddess pondered her next move, doing her best to measure her words the best way she could. "For now, let things play out for the rest of the weekend. If anything else turns up that makes you pause, make sure You let Me know so I can handle it before it gets out to the rest of the attendees, okay?"

We all nodded, taking a look at the clock. We only had an hour to get ready for the play party in one of the designated outdoor spaces set up for the weekend. Goddess rose from her chair, making sure she got her hugs and kisses in for all three of us, and even giving a reassuring hug to Jelani to let him know things were not as bad as they seemed. I wanted to be as optimistic as my Goddess, but only time would tell if her positive outlook on things would manifest themselves.

Once they left, I turned to amani with a slick smile on my face. I popped back in my Top space in an instant, insistent on finishing this weekend on a high note. "Get My outfit prepared for the party, baby. After you're done with that, I'm gonna need you to make Me come."

Chapter Twenty

SAJIRA

I was lost in my thoughts as the afternoon sun kissed my skin, doing my best to zone out into my own personal universe. In the midst of finding that next plane of subconsciousness, I found myself indulging in feeling every inch of my body, every curve, every crevice, and arousing myself with each sojourn across my landscape. It was a peaceful space, one I loved being in.

And then that peace found itself being disturbed in the worst way possible.

"With Your permission, may i speak with You, please, my Lady?"

Why, God, why? "That isn't a good idea, and you know the reason why."

I didn't bother to look down to acknowledge him, to do so would have given him reason to stick around longer than I wanted him to be there. I continued to keep my sleep mask over my face, doing my best to do what was necessary to stay in my zone. I wasn't about to get into a war of words with him, and I was convinced that was what he wanted.

"i'm not trying to cause any problems, i only want to offer

myself as a bottom for one of Your scenes tonight, if it will please You."

"I have a bottom for that, and I'm enjoying him immensely. your participation in My weekend is not required, nor is it desired. Besides, aren't you supposed to be in service to Mistress Blaze?"

"Yes, but She does not plan to scene tonight and She has given me permission to seek out a Top for the party, and i would be honored if You would top me tonight."

I took a deep breath and exhaled. This was becoming more than it needed to be, and I chastised myself for allowing it. "I'm not in the habit of repeating Myself. The answer is no."

All I was trying to do was indulge in a little bit of sunbathing on my balcony while I had a little bit of sunlight left to bronze my skin to glorious perfection before Jelani and I headed to the party. It was a quiet early evening, or so I thought, and I wanted to take advantage of the thoughts in my head. They weren't complicated, but they centered around a sexy ass bottom who'd been at my beck and call all weekend.

The more I thought about it, the more I felt like I wanted to find out if there was something more that he and I could explore once this weekend was over. I would have to go through the House protocol with regard to outside relationships, but I was thankful that Daddy wasn't the type to be down with the dreaded "OPP"—one penis policy—and he wouldn't object to it, as long as it didn't affect my surrender to him and Goddess.

I already had the pitch planned out in my head, explaining how I would be able to handle both without issue, down to the days of the week I could see him. I wasn't even bothered by the fact that he was younger than me; amani was the same age, and we got along like best friends—with benefits, of course. The more I thought about it, the more excited I got, and the possibilities could be endless for as long as it could be had.

Then this idiot had to come along and try to fuck up my vibe, and this was the second time that he'd managed to try to do that. Ugh.

"Real talk, Kitana—"

I snapped out of my thoughts in an instant. "you have no right to even refer to Me with *that* name anymore, lynx. I don't care if I'm in Top space or back in My original position within the House, say that name again, and I'll beat you where you stand."

"Damn, You ain't gotta be so hostile." He took a few steps back, giving me a curious look. "What is it, You're not getting it the way You're used to since we split up?"

"She's getting it pretty good, the last time i checked." Hearing Jelani's voice interrupt the conversation felt like a laser cutting through carbon fiber. It was a welcome tone to wash away the nauseating voice trying to beg his way back into my good graces. "If i recall correctly, you have a Domina you are currently serving, which means you shouldn't even be breathing in my Lady's direction. It's in your best interest to move along, or i'll *move* you along."

If I could have gotten any wetter in that moment, I would have been lying my ass off. Watching Jelani act like an Alpha male and staking his territory was something I didn't think I would be able to see outside of watching Daddy when he's like this. The rush was overwhelming as I continued to watch this play out.

lynx wasn't impressed by Jelani's show of force. "you might wanna stay out of grown folks' business, little boy. i get that you're enthralled with my ex-wife, but this truly doesn't concern you."

"Oh, but that's where you're wrong, my dude," Jelani's words became less submissive-like and more aggressive. No lie, I was loving every minute of it. "What we're not gonna do is sit out here doing this back and forth rah-rah when we both know that you don't have a leg to stand on. you've already fucked up one time by trying to slick your way into my Lady's cottage, and now you wanna complicate matters by catching a fade in broad daylight."

"Oh, and you think you man enough to shoot that fade?"

"you goddamn right, my dude. Don't let how we both identify fool you, and honestly, this ain't what you want. However, for my Lady's sake, i'm gonna give you a choice: you can walk away peacefully and we will forget any of this happened, or you can catch this fade and explain again to security how you decided that the warning against being in my Lady's space was beneath you."

Jelani's hands clenched into fists, staring lynx down like he wanted him to go ahead and take option number two. Hell, I was dying for him to do it because a little violence was good for the libido and a damn good aphrodisiac. I could have egged this on a little more for the entertainment value alone, but I decided enough was enough for now. "Jelani, be a good boy and get everything ready for the party tonight, please? I would hate for you to have to get dirty playing with street trash. I'll take care of him Myself with a little chat with his Mistress, and I don't mean the one he's pledged to for the weekend, either."

lynx's face lost all its color at the mere mention of Mistress Sinsual. I would have thought by now that he was tired of being in the doghouse, and if he kept it up, he would find himself on the outside looking in. His shoulders slumped, and he turned on his heel to trudge in the opposite direction, away from my cottage and toward the open-air dungeon.

Jelani looked up at me with the biggest smirk on his face. "You do know the paramedics would have had to carry him up out of here, right? i don't play about my commitments to those who deserve it…and You definitely deserve someone who has Your back for once."

I realized he was talking from the adrenaline and the bravado from causing lynx to back down, but I already had two men who had my back. Still, it was nice to have some backup in this moment. My body was doing its best to betray me, and the anger in my heart began to manifest itself into sexual heat. I decided to leave him to his ego for now, and take some pride in the fact that he defended my honor.

"Yes, I do, pretty boy. Now, bring your fine ass up here so we can get ready for this party. Tonight is going to be one for the books."

Chapter Twenty-One

NEFERTERRI

I was in the midst of putting my outfit together for the party tonight, when an unexpected knock at the front door of my cottage interrupted the vibe I was creating. I was waiting for Sigma to accompany me to the party, but once I looked at the clock, I realized he was a good half-hour earlier than I'd directed. I didn't have a problem with that, to be honest; I'd been edging him for the majority of the day, sexting with him to give him a sneak preview of what he might get a chance to sample if he did as he was told tonight.

I refused to hide the devious grin on my face as I padded toward the door to let him in. I'd been so busy in event programming mode that I hadn't had the chance to cut loose at all. That would end tonight, come hell or high water. I had every intention of wearing him out or wearing myself out in the process. Either way, I wanted every muscle to scream at me for pushing them past any predetermined limits.

That grin soon faded in the moments after I'd opened the door. "What in the hell are *You* doing here?"

"My Lady, I know I'm probably the last person You would want to see right now—"

"You have a gift for understatement, so, what in the hell are You doing here, again?"

Norene felt like she'd regretted whatever was in her head that convinced her that coming over here to see me was a good idea to try. "Lady Neferterri, I would like a word with You, in private, so that we can perhaps clear the air between us."

"Now, why would I want to do anything of the sort?" I rebutted. I crossed my arms over my chest as I regarded her guarded body language. It might have had something to do with the fact that I looked like I was ready to drag her within an inch of her life. "You tried My submissive, You questioned My ability to control and maintain dominion over My submissives, all but saying that I am not the Domina I *know* I am on several occasions. I'm still convinced that You're here to continue to undermine this event, but I was out-voted, otherwise You would be back in New York as we speak."

"You're right, My Lady."

I was in the process of laying out the other mental bullet points to further drive my point home when that little quip hit my ears. I almost stopped mid-sentence. "You wanna run that by Me again?"

Norene exhaled, resigning herself to the fact that she needed to repeat herself. "My Lady, everything that You've said cannot be denied. There are things that I am not entirely proud of, and others that I was, quite simply, flat out wrong about You."

I felt like I was in the *Twilight Zone* all over again. "Okay, woman, spill it, why are You here? What are You hoping to gain by this admission, My forgiveness? I'm not My Beloved. He may have His moments where He can be the ultimate diplomat and turn the other cheek, but it's going to take a hell of a lot more than words strung together to convince Me that You've somehow turned over a new leaf."

"I don't pretend to think that You would just forgive Me out of the blue, My Lady, but I needed to get this handled between us. There are too many things raging within Me that won't allow Me to rest until I found the nerve to apologize." Norene's eyes never left mine as she continued to purge. The way she looked at me made uncomfortable, though. "It's the only way I would be able to fully function the rest of this weekend. Whether You decided to forgive Me for the wrong I'd caused You and amani, I needed to do this."

"Okay, You've apologized, and I can't say that I accept Your apology, but I respect the courage to come here and take whatever heat I was going to give You for even being in such close proximity to Me, knowing how I feel about You."

"It doesn't compare to how I feel about You, My Lady." Norene's eyes took a sudden turn downward, throwing me for a complete loop. "The reason I gave You so much grief for so long is that, deep down, I've been intensely attracted to You. Even being in Your presence now makes Me want to drop to My knees and worship You."

What. The. Fuck? "Have You been drinking? Did You get high or something? Do You even know what You're saying to Me right now?"

I had to take a beat for a second to try to figure out what angle she was coming at me from. I looked at her like she'd grown a third eye, but the evil side of me crept into the mix. There might be a way to spin this in my favor, it was a matter of how to do it.

"Yes, I know what I'm saying, and it's taken Me a long time to reconcile it before even admitting it to You," she replied, doing her best to maintain some sort of calm the best way she knew how. "At the risk of sounding mildly masochistic, I wanted to subject Myself to an intense whipping by Your hand, to atone for My transgressions against You and Your House. I deserve every mark that You choose to leave on My skin."

"Wait, wait, You really are serious right now, aren't You?" I moved into her space, watching her tremble as I closed the distance between us. Oh, this was too precious for words! "So, what exactly did You have in mind for all of this to happen, Norene? Do You realize that You may put Yourself in harm's way by doing this?"

"Yes, My Lady, I'm well aware, but I can't deny how much You turn Me on. I'm willing to do whatever it takes to get back in Your good graces, anything to have Your hands on Me." Norene struggled to keep from touching any part of my body, acting like the very action of grazing my skin would result in an electric shock. "I want You, My Lady."

In that moment, I considered the possibilities. To get revenge for amani and me in one fell swoop was too good to pass up. I could even put the bitch on display in an outright humiliation scene to put the nail in the coffin of her public persona as a Domina as punishment for the shit she put me through. The thoughts in my head were so tempting that I almost said yes.

However, there was one thing that kept me from saying yes: I didn't want to lay one single, solitary finger on her body. Not. One. Finger. The thought repulsed me more than subjecting myself to the most brutal torture imaginable. No matter what I wanted to do to balance the scales, as my Beloved would say, there was no way in hell it was going to go down that way.

But that didn't mean it couldn't happen in a manner I saw fit, though. "I will see what can be done to facilitate this request. If I grant this request, it will be done how I see fit, and You will not object to how this will be carried out. Are we clear on this?"

"Yes, My Lady, we are clear. All I want is to make things right."

I closed the door as Norene left, leaning against the door to gather my thoughts and calm myself as much as I could. Tonight would be more daunting than I thought it would be, and it would take some savvy to pull everything off. In order to do that, I was going to have to enlist the help of my bestie, and with the way she felt about Norene, I had a sneaky suspicion that she would consider this an early Christmas gift.

Chapter Twenty-Two

NEFERTERRI

It wasn't hard to figure out who I needed to see ASAP. My only hope was that she wasn't already otherwise engaged. I'd left her with another special project to handle as she saw fit, and it provided me with the opportunity to get an update on how that project was going.

I knocked on the door to her cottage, checking my watch to make sure I had time to sit for a minute, in case what I saw would cause an elongated conversation. Imagine my surprise when I saw Earl opening the door while on all fours. He'd had a mouth bit covering his mouth, preventing him from speaking. In the distance, I could hear Sin yelling at him in her typical aggression.

"slave, is that Lady Neferterri at the door? Grunt once for yes, twice for no!"

Earl did as he was told, acknowledging my presence with enough volume that she could hear his audible response. If I was a more compassionate Domina, I would have felt sorry for whatever the hell he had to subject himself to while dealing with whatever torture tactics Sin had at her disposal. However, in light of recent events, I pretty much deduced that whatever she had him doing, it was its own version of next-level madness.

I followed Earl as he crawled into the living area, where I saw Sin lounging and relaxing like she didn't have a care in the world. "There's My bestie. Come, sit down, indulge a bit. I'm happy to see You."

I kissed both her cheeks before I took my seat in one of the lounge chairs. Earl dropped at Sin's feet, picked up a book that had me do a double-take over why he was reading it. The book was *The New Jim Crow* by Michelle Alexander.

Cue the pin-drop moment. "What in the world do You have this slave doing for You?"

She looked down at the other books in the pile of books and smiled. "A good friend of Mine gave Me the idea a while back whenever it came to white male submissives that She felt needed to be rehabilitated. Her motivation was financial; Mine is rooted in My usual love of psychological sadism."

She felt Earl flinch for a moment as he continued to read, prompting her to jab her heel into his lower back. "Is there a reason that you're moving when I have not sanctioned it, slave? Are you feeling some discomfort over what you're reading? Grunt once for yes, twice for no."

Earl grunted twice the best way he could, considering he was in pain from the point of the heel digging into his flesh. After a few more minutes, Sin took the heel off his back and rested her legs on top of his back again. "If you flinch again because something has you thinking you should be reacting to it negatively, I'll have you whipped within an inch of your life. Are we clear?"

Earl grunted once to acknowledge her question before settling back to read the book he had been tasked with. Sin's face never changed from its stoic demeanor as she glowered over him. "Good, let's ensure that it doesn't happen again the rest of this weekend if you want to be back in your Mistress's good graces. I don't know why She would want you back anyway, you're not worth the energy I'm burning to put you back in place."

I sat in my chair, in observation mode, taking what I want and leaving the rest on the shelf. There have always been various methodologies when it came to authority transfer dynamics, although the more mainstream term was power exchange. Some loved the "iron fist" strategy, while others loved the more nuances coercion tactics that would have the bottom or submissive seduced into their surrender.

As much as I might have been revered in some instances, my best friend reveled in being feared. Real talk, we were both comfortable with that.

"So, I'm assuming Your visit has something to do with a couple of issues popping up inside the compound, yes?" Sin got straight to the point, ignoring the footstool beneath her like he was nothing more than the piece of organic furniture he was meant to be in that moment.

"Among other things, yes." I was always amazed at how she was able to read my body language in an instant. That empathic part of her was something I could relate to, but it irked me beyond comprehension when it was pointed in my direction. "I was visited by Lady Norene, and She presented Me with a rather unorthodox proposal."

Sin tried her best to wipe the smirk off her face. "She tried You, didn't She? That twit has no conscience, I swear. So, what are You going to do, or is that the reason You're here? You want Me to handle that for You?"

"Yep."

"It must be Christmas somewhere in the world. My birthday isn't for another six months!" She looked like a woman who would have danced all over her cottage and praised the gods for whatever favor they had bestowed upon her. "You can't be serious? She really put Herself on the chopping block? For what?"

"I'm trying to wrap My head around it, and the only thing I can think of is that She has an angle I'm not thinking about." I was still skeptical; I couldn't trust her as far as I could throw her. "I still feel like She's done something and She's trying to use this as some sort of leverage in case whatever She tried to get away with blows up in Her face."

"I'm gonna be honest with You, bestie. I don't care! She needs to be dropped a notch or two," she replied. "I haven't forgotten what She did to You back then, and I've been dying to find a way to get back for that. Now You're telling Me that She's basically turned Herself into a sacrificial lamb on the altar of the Church of Sadists and Primals. Say the word, and I'm there."

I sort of figured she would go for it, but I didn't expect her to be this gung ho about it, either. She did mention something that had my attention, and we needed to flesh that out, too. "What other stuff has been going on, Sis? The way You responded to My request has Me wondering if there's something I'm missing out on."

Sin's eyes narrowed, her brow furrowed to match her anger, and she dropped the bombshell I didn't see coming. "Blaze has betrayed both of us."

"What the hell are You talking about?"

"She's made legitimate offers to our respective properties,

releasing Jelani in the process after one of my considered properties accepted Her proposal." Sin looked like she was more saddened than she was angered. "After ten years, You would have thought She wouldn't have wanted to throw it all away like this."

"Wait…wait…so, You're telling Me that She tried to sway My amani?" I stood up with the intent to head to the door to lay waste to anyone and anything in my path to get to Blaze. *So, this was what her attitude was about?* "I'll kill Her."

"Slow down, Sis. I need You to take a breath. After all, I'm the one who lost property in this whole clusterfuck. If anyone should be setting a nuclear bomb off, it should be Me."

I stopped in my tracks once I realized that she had a point. I sat down in my chair, still trying to calm myself. "Why on Earth would She do this to either of us? What did She hope to gain? She had to know that this would all but end things between us, right?"

"I don't know what Her motivations were, but I plan to find out tomorrow when I bring Her up on those charges to the Council. Since Hatshepsut and paka are here, they can mediate until we come to a conclusion."

"Blaze couldn't have been in Her right mind."

"I love Your propensity for looking on the bright side of things, Neferterri. It's one of the things I've always loved about You." Sin's body language resembled a stone-like reserve. She was beginning to scare me. "When She is censured and removed from the Council and banned from the compounds, I am going to look Her in the eyes and ask Her if it was worth it."

I wasn't sure if I wanted to believe it, but the pieces were coming together. Blaze had avoided us almost the whole weekend, hasn't said two words outside of the contentious stares between us at the beginning of the event. At this point, she was no less of an enemy than Lady Norene herself. I wanted to be wrong, but there was no way to tell if I would be or not.

I put that out of my mind in order to reset my focus for tonight's indulgences. I couldn't afford to be distracted or to let on that I might know. "Okay, Sis, let's leave it out in the dungeon tonight, enjoy everything we set out to do. In the morning, we handle business. Is that good for You?"

"As our younger boys love to say—say no more, bestie. I got You. Now, let's go fuck some shit up."

Chapter Twenty-Three

SHAMISE

The funny part about being on the left side of the slash was that it brought you a perspective you didn't want to see. It also brings all types of things to your doorstep that you didn't want to deal with all the time. It was one of the few times I never envied Daddy or Goddess; I enjoyed my love of serving and surrendering to them, and letting them handle the stuff that was above my station.

Whenever I felt like I needed to unload, I always loved being able to do it with sajira or tiger, and even the past few weeks I'd been able to confide in amani with a few things. There were others, but they didn't share the bond that the four of us shared. I needed to do something about expanding my circle, but if I was honest with myself, I couldn't trust these women as far as I could throw them.

Seeing tiger at my front door was a bit of a shock to the system. He looked like he was ready to burst, and from the way he kept bouncing around, it didn't look like a regular social call. "Okay, you don't look all that well, honey. Is there something wrong?"

"shamise, baby, i need to request some free time to speak,

and i need it now, with Your permission, please? Some shit done went down and it needs to be addressed and then some."

There were two things that required a full stop from any protocol adherence whenever tiger and I were around each other: when a secret needed to be revealed or when something dangerous was about to befall someone close to either of us. I already began to feel the hairs on the back of my neck stand up based on the look on his face alone.

I pulled him into the room within seconds as I tried to figure out what had him so spooked. amani raced into the room when he heard the stress in tiger's voice, his body tensing in anticipation of whatever was about to be divulged. We walked with him to the couch, where they took their positions at my feet while I curled up on the cushions to brace for impact.

Once we settled in, tiger exhaled and got himself together before he dropped the bombshell. "Mistress and Mistress Blaze got into it late last night. Well, it was like around five this morning, but whatever. She's losing out on Jelani worrying about fucking lynx, and Mistress is tripping out big time."

I cocked my head to the side, trying to get a gauge on the situation the best way I knew how. "Wait, I thought that lynx was being drummed out anyway, why should She care what happens to lynx now?"

"Mistress still has a soft spot for his dumb ass, i don't know." He shrugged his shoulders, doing his best to slow himself down long enough to get the crux of the stuff he ear-hustled. "The thing that baffles me is why Mistress Blaze is trying it with Mistress anyway. She knows that woman has a temper and Her eruptions would make Mount St. Helens look like a small firecracker going off."

"Maybe Mistress Blaze has gotten to the point to where She doesn't care anymore," amani chimed in. He paused for a minute to explain himself, not quite sure if he wanted to say what was on his mind next. "So, you both know all that madness that happened on the island when i came to Goddess's rescue, right? Well, Mistress Blaze kinda started flirting with me once we got back Stateside, usually in passing whenever we were out at different events, which was why I was so uncomfortable around Her during the Marketplace session."

To say I was heated was an understatement. "Why didn't you tell Me or sajira about this? We would have gone through the channels to have that handled."

amani shrugged, which let me know that he was still new to handling rebuffing Dominants, regardless of gender. "i kinda figured it would have, you know, gone away on its own. She had Jelani, and i know he's had Her attention—or at least, i thought he did. Besides, i didn't want to worry Goddess about it, She was working so hard to make this event successful, i didn't want to seem like a burden or anything."

"What about Daddy?"

"Sir has been in and out of the country, and when He's been home, He and Dom have been dealing with the stuff at the security firm," amani explained. "So, i dealt with it on my own."

I caressed his face, seeing the weight of the world on his shoulders and realizing that we hadn't been able to help with that in any way. "I had no idea you were dealing with this, why didn't you feel comfortable enough to tell us, baby? you're just as important to them as your sis and I are, I know you know that."

"Yes, but i'm still used to handling my own battles. Ever since that mess with Lady Norene, i felt like i was helpless, bound by freaking protocol and having our Dominants handle things. That's not how i was brought up."

"I understand that. One of Daddy's brothers always loved to say, "Standing alone doesn't mean you are alone, it means you are strong enough to handle things all by yourself." I've seen you handle things, but I don't ever want you to think that you have to handle things on your own. It's not about being capable or not, it's about being able to trust family when the time is needed."

"Oh, and that means me, too, while you over there playing like we're not family," tiger interjected. "i don't claim a lot of people in this life, so you're stuck with my fabulous ass."

amani laughed for the first time during our conversation. "i hear you, tiger, but i still would like to believe that i can stand on my own two feet when the situation calls for it. There are times when i feel like i'm helpless. Who wants that in a submissive?"

I smiled, looking into his eyes as he tried to break from my loving stare. "Listen to me, pretty boy, and tiger can attest to this, tool: you are not helpless. you have always been resourceful, you think on your feet, and you protect what's yours. But what our Dominants handle among themselves is based on information that we provide to them so they can keep from going off half-cocked."

"But, my Lady—"

"Shh, no buts, baby. I've been around them long enough to know that, even if you think you're hiding something, they always find a way to find out. There's no hiding from either of them, so why try?" I watched his eyes as he nodded his understanding of what I was telling him. "If this is bothering you, it's bothering all of us, baby, and if it bothers them, you and I both know it will get handled in ways we hardly imagine. Remember the incident resolution on the island if you need a reminder. They still haven't found those two for what they tried to do to Daddy and Goddess."

The smirk on amani's face was enough confirmation for me to relax a little, but I still needed to figure out what to do about tiger. "If Mistress Blaze is going off the reservation and Mistress Sin isn't going for it, eventually it will get to Goddess. What do you think we need to do to avoid the mother of all clashes, tiger? Or do we sit back and let it happen and pick up the pieces afterward?"

"Look, girlie, the last thing we need to do is get in the midst of lionesses when they got beef that needs to be handled," tiger replied. He mocked washing his hands of the situation as he pondered his next words. "Here's the deal: we need to roll with this and let the chips fall where they may. That means You and amani continue to enjoy each other, let Your sis and Jelani do what they're doing, and i'm going to focus on making sure Lady Hatshepsut tells Her people in Vegas that She had a fucking good time so that we can all do this again next year, capiche?"

I almost wanted to laugh at his loose usage of Italian to get his point across, but that's the wildest part of dealing with tiger. Even while he's being dead serious, he has to find some comedy to help lighten the mood. "Okay, but the minute it starts to affect any of us, we drop the hammer, does that work?"

"Sounds good to me," amani remarked. "i'm just glad i don't have to carry all this around anymore. i promise to come to You or sajira if something is bothering me. You two are like big sisters to me, even if we are sexual a lot of the time."

"Oh, hush, you enjoy it too much to be complaining about it, bruh." tiger waved his hand in his usual dismissive manner, not trying to hear amani's feigned distaste for indulging with sajira and me. "So, now that that's out of the way, what are You wearing to the party tonight, my Lady? You know i can't have You looking all rag-tag and basic, and that goes for Your sis, too. i'll be stopping by Her cottage as soon as i'm done with You to get her snatched and right."

Chapter Twenty-Four

SAJIRA

As I was luxuriating in the bubble bath Jelani drew for me after we'd dismissed lynx from my personal universe, my thoughts drifted to the party later tonight. I soaped my body from head to toe, inhaling the combined scents of vanilla, cinnamon and chamomile lavender that served to surge my libido into inferno-level heat, pondering what debauchery he and I could find ourselves in by the end of the night. We needed this in ways I couldn't describe.

I'd sent him out into the compound to secure our scening area so I could have some time to myself to fully immerse in the sexiness of the atmosphere. I closed my eyes, allowing every sensual desire to flood my mind, when other decadent memories unleashed themselves into my psyche, whether I wanted them to or not. Almost like they'd happened yesterday, interludes that my ex-husband and I engaged in with other women and men found themselves playing out like classic movies—or more like horror movies, looking back on it now.

I felt stupid for the way my body felt whenever he popped in my mind like that. Sex was never the problem between us; if anything, I could separate my heart and my libido and fuck him into oblivion without a second thought. But what he did to me was unforgivable. He lied about his sexuality for God knows how long, and expected me to take the blame for not seeing it for myself and accepting it without question. I resolved that even if my body wanted the release, what might have been good for my sexual health wasn't good for my mental health.

I wiped my thoughts from those problematic images and focused harder on what I wanted in the now as I caressed my body, imagining Daddy's hands all over me. God, the mere thoughts of him seemed to make everything disappear so that there was nothing left to see except him. I could hear him whispering in my ear, telling me not to worry about lesser men who didn't deserve the platinum between my thighs, making me giggle over how naughty it made me feel, putting me back in the mood I wanted to be in by the time Jelani got back from handling my errand. *Reason...season...lifetime. There's a reason he isn't in my life anymore, and there is a reason Jelani is here now.*

I looked up from my self-indulgence to find Jelani kneeling by the tub, much to my delight. I sensed a bit of calm in him as he knelt there, but there was a sense of trepidation, too. When I dried my hand off to caress his cheek, he gave up a half-smile, never looking up to meet my gaze. His body language was guarded, which put me on alert. "Are you okay, baby? Did something happen while you were out? Were you unable to get the space I requested?"

"Yes, my Empress, i was able to get the space You requested." He sounded so robotic, like something took some of his joy away. "May i go into the other room so i can get Your outfit together?"

"No, you may not." I was used to him trying to touch me, even if he had to get permission to do it, and it disturbed me that he hadn't done it since reentering my personal space. "Jelani, what happened, talk to Me."

Jelani's shoulders slumped, shaking his head like he was trying to decide if he should say something. "my Empress, Mistress Blaze tried to have a conversation with me while I was in the open dungeon area."

"What did She say? Did She say something to you that cause you to look like you do right now?" I didn't know what came over me, but I was in protective mode, ready to jump out of the tub and rip Blaze a new one.

"Mistress expressed to me that once this weekend was over, i could consider myself released from Her consideration. She said that She'd heard about some of the things i was doing for You this weekend and felt like i was putting more into You than i was doing for Her." He looked confused, like he didn't understand why she would have made such a claim.

The anger rose, but I kept it under wraps for a minute. "She couldn't possibly have found out about anything happening between us. I made sure of that. Did She say where She heard the information?"

"She wouldn't commit, only saying She had a "trusted source" or something like that," he replied. "To be honest, i think i have a clue who She might have been listening to, and if i'm right, i'm gonna hurt him, real talk. Forgive me for sounding so aggressive, my Empress, but i didn't do anything wrong."

"No, you didn't, baby, and I have a feeling I know who's been feeding Her, too," I mused, my anger reaching a fevered pitch with each passing second. "Allow Me to handle that, and

I plan to get My sis involved with that, too. I'm sick and tired of his manipulative ass."

I got out of the tub and dried off, wrapping the towel around my body as I headed to the bedroom to get my cellphone. I sent a text to shamise, hoping that she was still in her cottage to answer the text. *That son of a bitch of an ex of mine just got Jelani released over BS. Need to chat ASAP. Can You come over?*

Within seconds, her response was enough to send me through the roof. *Sounds like a lot of fuckery is going on. Mistress Blaze just tried our little brother, trying to convince him that Goddess wants to drop him for Jelani.*

The next series of texts between us opened up all sorts of revelations from tiger, too, and by the time we were done cross-referencing stories, it was decided that we needed to take our concerns to Goddess as soon as possible. The only problem was that we were still supposed to be in event protocol until Sunday afternoon when all property was being returned to their rightful owners.

Jelani looked like he was more concerned about my agitated state than I was concerned about what he was going through. "my Empress, is everything okay? Who needs to bleed? How can i make things less stressful for You?"

I smiled, realizing he'd forgone his own pain to worry about what was happening with me, when I was the one trying to ease his pain by removing the worries from his mind. It was an endearing moment, but for now, I had to be the one to take the reins and make sure we were both good. It was what Goddess would do. "Listen to Me, pretty boy, what Mistress did to you had nothing to do with you, but we're going to find a way to make it right. I don't blame you if you don't want to deal with Her anymore, but I got you, okay?"

Jelani raised an eyebrow, unsure of what I was referring to. In that moment, I understood why Daddy and Goddess try to explain to us that some things are not meant for us to worry over. "Just tell me what i need to do to ensure that tonight is everything You want it to be, and I will concentrate on that. It will take my mind off all the bullshit, and it might make me better for someone who can appreciate what i can bring to the table."

I nodded, stroking his cheek as I pulled his eyes up to look at me. I kissed him soft and slow, running the risk of igniting my body and not caring if we made it to the party or not. His body felt like it was made for mine, my only all-consuming thought was to sex away every problem we both had. "Baby, you bring a lot to the table, anyone could see that. Well, almost anyone. I have a feeling you will be much better off with someone who is better suited to appreciate your specific…talents."

"i hope so, my Empress."

His confidence was shaken, I could feel it on him, and it irritated me, putting me in a position to where I needed to do whatever it took to insist that the opposite was true. It was hard enough to get submissive men to come out and be in a public forum, and I was not about to sit by and allow one who had so much raw potential go to waste. In fact, a plan sprang up in that moment, and I needed to talk to my sis as soon as possible. Not only did we have to put the screws to Mistress Blaze, but there was another proposal I needed her and amani's support on. I just hoped they were down for it.

Chapter Twenty-Five

SAJIRA

My mind was all over the place as I headed to reserve the area where sajira and I would scene later tonight, and that was an honest understatement. So many things were happening in such a short period of time, it was a dizzying prospect to recount it all in my head. I was worried about my frat; I didn't want him thinking that I had designs on his Domina. I was happy right where I was, despite my separation anxiety.

While it had been less than two full days since I'd seen Goddess, it was affecting me more than I thought it would. Being on the compound and not having access to her felt like I was being punished for something, even though I wasn't being punished at all. I asked to be a part of this weekend, after all; I could have sat this one out, but that alternative was even more unbearable. shamise was awesome as my Top for the weekend, but even she recognized that despite her best efforts, she wasn't our Goddess.

I needed to be in her space, to feel her energy and have it consume me, balance me. I didn't want to feel the way I felt, but I couldn't help myself. I felt needy, and I felt guilty for feeling needy; the other submissives sort of waltzed around like it was another day at the office, while I was acting like an addict in need of his next fix. The constant tug-of-war pulling me between what I wanted and what I needed was driving me crazy.

I got a glimpse of Goddess as she was making the final arrangements for tonight's festivities. She looked up for a moment and saw me staring at her like a lovesick puppy. She looked so stunning that I swore she began to emanate this golden aura around her. I continued to stare at her, hoping she would hear my silent plea to be near her, if only for a few brief moments.

She looked up again, smiling as she blew a kiss in my direction. I thought I would faint on the spot as I read her lips. *I miss my pretty boy, too. The minute this is over, I promise I'm gonna wear you out.*

To say that would have kept me floating for at least another week didn't do her small gesture justice. Now I understood why my sisters got all googly-eyed when Sir would give them that "look" when he needed them to be patient a little while longer. She was twenty feet away from me and without a single touch, she got me righteous again. I felt like I could handle anything that came my way.

Too bad it wouldn't last but a few seconds. "Hi, gorgeous, how is your weekend going so far? Have you been having any fun?"

There weren't too many things that I couldn't deal with, and I took pride in being able to adjust to the unexpected. The problem with the unexpected was that I couldn't deal with the triggers until the triggers were placed in front of me for me to deal with. Only then would I know whether I could handle myself as well as I thought I could. This particular trigger was one that I chose not to deal with, and it threatened to knock me off my square.

"Good evening to You, Lady Norene. To what do i owe the unexpected interruption of my thoughts?" I was supposed to maintain discipline, but she rattled my nerves something awful. "Forgive me for being rude, but i need to get back to my Lady to get Her ready for tonight."

"Aw, don't be in such a hurry, amani," she replied, taking hold of my forearm to stop me from walking away. "I only wanted to chat, to make sure your head is in the right place. I saw you flirting with your Goddess, and I have to say I'm impressed with your dedication to Her, despite what I've been hearing about Her wanting to replace you."

God forgive me for entertaining this twit, but I did it anyway to get her out of my space once and for all. "Indulge me with the rumors that You've been hearing, my Lady. It should be worth a good laugh or two."

Lady Norene frowned as she pulled out her smartphone. She tried to be discreet, but she was in direct violation of the rules of the event. "Take a look at your *Goddess* with Her head of security and tell Me if I'm hearing things."

The video must have been no longer than thirty seconds, but the audio must have been what she thought she was supposed to get my anger up over. The audio caught Goddess lusting over how much Sigma turned her on and how she'd been wanting to get her hands on him for a long time and all the other sexy talk that I'd heard her speak about other submissives since we'd been together. I couldn't say it didn't unnerve me; I hadn't seen Goddess conduct herself quite like this, but I wasn't about to give this idiot the satisfaction of thinking her efforts were having their desired effect.

Lady Norene's smile began to creep back on her face as she continued to try to read my blank expression. Once the video ended, the smile turned into a smirk. "I don't know about you, but I would never treat My property with such disrespect. It flies in the face of how things are supposed to be between Domina and submissive. I mean, I would expect that type of behavior from your Sir; you men can't exactly help yourselves, but I thought your Goddess carried Herself with a little more class than that."

I didn't know what happened to me in that moment, but it felt like a switch had flipped in my head. In one minute, I wanted to rip through her with the ferocity of a Rottweiler, leaving nothing left for her to put together. I felt the heat rising through me, the anger seeming to consume me whole, causing this irrational behavior that I knew wasn't becoming, and threatened to undo all the training Goddess had invested in me.

In the next minute, my focus returned to my Goddess. I could hear her voice in my ear, telling me that I was better than this, that there was a way to handle this without flying off the handle. *Surgical strikes always work better than dropping bombs, baby boy, and they don't leave as big a mess, either.*

I closed my eyes for a few more moments, ignoring whatever it was that Lady Norene was trying to say to me, centering my core, remembering my lessons. I knew what I needed to do, and it was going to be fun doing it, too. I didn't want to come out of my face with the next few things that came out of my mouth, but she'd gone too far. Goddess would have to understand. "You do know that my Dominants are polyamorous, yes?"

"Yes, I know that, but what does that have to do with—"

"—and since they are polyamorous, Goddess and Sir don't

have a problem with being upfront and honest when it comes to who they might be interested in scening with, yes?"

"Yes, but I don't see what that has to—"

She was running into a buzz saw and she had no clue it was coming. "Now, since You *know* that my Dominants are poly, upfront and honest about their desires, and You *know* that they also encourage us to be as upfront and honest about ours, logic would dictate that there is not a damn thing You could show me that would change that narrative?"

Lady Norene's demeanor changed, and so did her tone. "I don't know why I bother with you low-rent submissive men anyway. I only came down here to—"

"To what, try to see if You could drive a wedge between a Domina and her *committed* and *owned* property? Especially when that *committed* and *owned* property is also polyamorous, right?" I guessed I was wearing the collar around my neck for shits and giggles or something. The Kemi-Ka crest pendant dangling from the O-ring on my collar must have been smudged or covered in dirt and grime, otherwise she would have seen it as plain as day. "Do Yourself a favor and excuse Yourself from conversing with me again. And in case You needed a reminder, this will get reported to the Council the minute we disengage."

Lady Norene sneered at me, trying to intimidate me, but I was beyond that possibility now. "you don't have the leverage to pull that off, you sorry excuse for a submissive. It will be My word against yours, and since your Goddess will have to recuse Herself from the hearing, you won't have anyone who can tip the scales for you."

"Then, there's nothing for *You* to worry about, right?" She seemed a bit confused over my bravado, but it wasn't for her to try and understand. "Again, walk away, before i really forget my training. After all, i am supposed to represent my House with respect, and i would hate to break from House protocol because someone who was told to not engage me unless one of my Dominants was present decided that She didn't have enough respect for them to honor that request."

Lady Norene walked away without another word spoken, looking disturbed over how the encounter turned out. It was safe to say that she thought she had the upper hand, but what she tended to forget was that not everyone operated in the shadows. We learned that lesson after what happened on the island and the subsequent conversations we had as a House based upon those who walked in darkness, trying to break Sir and Goddess apart.

I meant what I said, I was about to blow up her spot and showcase her sneaky ass for the whole Council to see. By the time they were done with her, she was going to wish all she did was try to sway my sense of loyalty. Rules have been broken, and there were consequences to those actions.

I shook the negativity off my body and mind and headed back to the cottage so I could help shamise get prepared for the party. I couldn't wait to see what could possibly happen tonight, but one thing was for certain: fun, in every sense of the word, was the word of the night.

The minute I got back to the cottage, shamise could tell I was disturbed. I didn't bother to hide it, either; after our conversation about trust, there was no point in doing too much to put a mask over it all. I tried my best to verbalize it, but my shock and anger took over and silenced me more than I'd wanted to be. "sis...Norene...She tried—"

She didn't say too much in response, she simply wrapped

her arms around me and kissed my cheek. "I could feel it on you the moment you stepped through the door. Do I need to end Her?"

I found my voice, and the volume to go with it. I was not about to sound like I was meek and without my own power. I was better than that. "She's gone too far, my Lady. She insulted Goddess. She tried me, thought i would betray Goddess over something trivial."

"Shhh, it will be fine. We will handle all of this, and things will calm down and we will be able to balance things out again." She sounded so soothing, like warm honey being dripped all over me. "Now, let's get things together and prepare to show up and show out tonight. Sounds good?"

I slipped out of her embrace, heading to the bedroom to get the bags together for the party. "i'm with you, my Lady. We need to get some things out of our system before handling business in the morning."

Chapter Twenty-Six

NEFERTERRI

I struggled with my emotions for the first time in a long time as Norene sat in a chair across from me, zip-tied down, opened and vulnerable. In order for me to be able to pull this off, I was going to have to get myself together, but the mere sight of her made my blood boil. I wished I could make her disappear, but there wasn't much I could do to make that happen without incurring a few illegalities. Beloved would kill me.

"You go through the circles we all run in, thinking You're so much better than the rest of us. I bet You're convinced that we're not on Your level in any shape or form, aren't You?"

"That's not true, I—"

"I didn't say You could talk!" I wanted to reach into the darkest depths of my mind, to find that evilness that so many wanted to attribute to me whenever they crossed me. To unleash that would be a needed relief. "I'm going to shut You up, one way or another."

This was supposed to play out as a humiliation scene, something I'd abhorred in the past, but my motivations were different then. Now, I wanted to grind her into nothingness, but not before I had a little sadistic fun in the process.

We were in the comfort of the master bedroom inside the main building, an area that was deemed off limits by anyone except for me, Beloved, and Amenhotep. Having that extra layer of privacy to pull this off was a delectable prospect for me, albeit a scarier one for the woman sitting in front of me. The fear in her eyes was tangible, but one that I no longer possessed the capacity to extend any compassion over.

Her eyes conveyed the shock in how much bitterness was tinged in every word I hurled in her direction. Maybe it was a kink scene for her to get her rocks off and somehow earn my forgiveness in the same stroke, but this was more of an exorcism for me. As with any exorcism, someone was going to suffer from the extraction of the demons.

"You know what? I guess I should see what You have to work with before I even allow You the honor of being touched by Me."

The shock on her face was priceless. She looked like she wanted to back out of her agreement, and I almost gave her a reason to when I took one of my knives from its sheath in my bag and headed toward her. "Wha…what are You going to do with that?"

"That is none of Your concern, especially when You've been dying to be such a good little bitch for Me, haven't You?"

Norene's eyes widened as she struggled in the chair, doing her best to keep from reacting to the phrase I'd spoken. She shook her head in a violent manner, her eyes viewing me with every ounce of contempt she could muster before she went under. I was waiting for that moment to occur so I could begin.

What she hadn't counted on was my calling her contacts in New York to find out a good bit of information—including the

Top who she had been "secretly" bottoming for. In her outdated mind, she felt that it would somehow lessen her influence or something like that. I knew several Dominas who bottomed who garnered respect regardless, but for some reason she decided it was something she should hide.

All it did was give me something to hold over her head and exploit.

Her eyes were glazed over, giving me the opening I needed to begin my suggestive play on her mind. I took the knife and cut the zip-ties from her arms and legs. "Strip."

She struggled for a moment, her eyes looking through me instead of at me, but she soon began to strip her clothing. In the midst of it all, I could read her body language; part of her wanted to fight what was happening to her, but she didn't have a choice in the matter. Before long, her clothing was in a heap on the floor in front of me.

She did her best to try to cover herself as different parts of her consciousness were in conflict with each other. It was something I was familiar with, considering my dealings in erotic hypnosis. I took great care not to screw with her mind in a manner that would cause permanent harm, but I was so tempted to break from that promise to myself. She needed to be returned to herself and those in her charge, and I didn't want her in a diminished capacity. As much as I loathed her, I didn't wish to cause any irreparable harm.

Still, it was fun to watch her squirm. "Well, let's see, I don't think trying to cover Yourself like this is going to work. Now, here is how this is going to work: I'm going to blindfold You and do everything I want to do, and then I'm going to leave. I won't say a single word to You, I'm not going to allow You to say a word to Me, and when we're done here, I will consider

Your apology accepted. Nod Your understanding."

She nodded, not daring to incur any further wrath from me before I took the blindfold and tied it around her head. "Once I'm done with You, I will have the service submissives assist You back to Your cottage, where You will await a call with the phrase that will restore You to Your original state."

Once she was deprived of her visual senses, I headed to the door and opened it, taking care to not alert Norene to its distinct sound. Her senses would be heightened now that her sight had been taken from her. If I pulled this off, it would be some of my most intense work yet. Considering she'd never felt my hands before, she would never pick up on my deception.

I brought Sin into the room, allowing her to sit on the bed. I smiled as I watched my plan come to fruition. I nodded as I mouthed the words to prepare for what she'd had in mind to do to her as I guided her to get on all fours. Once I had her in position, I sat in a chair in an opposite corner to watch it all unfold in front of me.

Sin rose to her feet, licking her lips at the sight of her prey. She slid her fingers inside of her bare legs, grazing them against Norene's supple skin. It was a surprise, noticing how alluring she was. I nodded my head in Sin's direction as she prepared to dig in.

She grabbed the crop from the wall, landing it swift and hard against her ass, grinning as Norene twitched from the sensation. She strained against her mental bonds, wanting to run from the foreign pain being inflicted on her. She didn't dare run, but I could feel it on her with each swing from Sin. It was its own catharsis for me, feeling like an out-of-body experience, and I loved every minute of it.

The next series of swats came from her bare hand, each successive smack harsher than the former. She traced the end of the crop against Norene's body, popping it hard in strategic spots with the intent of making her jump. If the end result was to leave her in a pile of her own pain-soaked repentance, then Sin was getting close to that goal with every bit of skill and temperance necessary. She switched to one of the wooden paddles to continue her work, it was almost like something came over her, taking over for the restraint she'd shown up to this point.

With precision and near lethal force, Sin rained strokes of the paddle against the back of her thighs, her ass, focusing on those areas that would do nothing more than cause the type of searing pain that would serve as a reminder for some time to come. She heard the restrained whimpers coming from Norene, but it wasn't enough to satisfy her sadistic passions. If anything, they served to fuel her desires to continue to inflict the pain she wanted, coming ever so close to the edge of harming her.

Norene continued to do her best to keep from yelling out as the line between pleasure and pain continued to blur, finding that exercise futile as her endorphins got the best of her, forcing the moans and yells from her lips with such a savagery that I wondered if she would turn feral. Watching the scene intensify to its conclusion aroused me to the point of no return. I was going to have to relieve this tension the first chance I got, and I knew who I was going to take that tension out on.

Sin gave the signal that she was done with her, and from the looks of it, Norene would remember it for quite some time. She bore so many different hues on different parts of her body that she looked like a multicolored zebra. I wanted to laugh, but I had to maintain some semblance of decorum. She was supposed to be earning my forgiveness, after all.

I walked Sin to the door, kissing her on the cheek and mouthing a thank you before leaving the door cracked so the noise of the door shutting didn't disturb the space. I headed back to Norene, who was a crumpled heap on the floor, sobbing and laughing at the same time as the endorphins began to dissipate and reality settled in.

I was a woman of my word, but I wanted her to remember everything that happened to her in that moment. Call it the ultimate act of sadism, but I considered it presenting her with a pyrrhic victory of sorts. She might have gotten what she wanted, but it was going to come at a cost.

Before I left my bedroom to summon the submissives to take her to her cottage to recover from her demanding scene on both physical and emotional levels, I leaned down and whispered the trigger phrase to bring her out of the hypnosis she had been in the entire time. The rush of memories of what had befallen her would be a constant reminder. I wasn't about to allow her to think it was all a dream.

I wanted her to relive the horrors in the darkness over and over again, so much so that the mere sight of me would roil her stomach to the point to where she wouldn't want to be around me ever again in her wretched life. I spoke my final words after lifting her blindfold and hood to allow her to reorient her senses, making sure she saw my eyes as I spoke them.

"Consider Your apology accepted."

Chapter Twenty-Seven

SAJIRA

We weren't ten minutes inside of the open-air dungeon space in the courtyard when the pre-party shenanigans began.

I was in the midst of engaging with different people, enjoying the interactions for the most part, while Jelani was communing with the rest of the submissives. I had every intention of reclaiming him the first chance I got, laughing over my hidden low-key possessive streak over someone who I couldn't own. Didn't stop me from wanting to fantasize over the possibility.

That was before my fantasies were ripped from me in the blink of an eye. "Good evening, my Lady. You look absolutely gorgeous tonight."

"Step away now, and I won't lose My mind and find the nearest pair of knives and show you what my Daddy taught Me."

"Damn, still hostile? i could have sworn the young buck blew Your back out by now or something to calm all that down."

This was becoming more of a chore than I was willing to endure. "Whether he did or didn't is no longer a part of your circle of concern, jackass. Now, final warning, step away before something bad happens to you."

"You still don't get it, do You? You don't have what it takes to do anything to me."

Before I could follow through on his false show of bravado, he got rushed from the side, taken from my field of vision for a moment or two. The next thing I knew, Jelani was in his face, looking like a panther unleashed from its cage. His stance was overaggressive, to the point to where a circle formed around them by instinct, with the anticipation of a confrontation that made *Fight Club* look like a sparring exhibition.

"i told you not to come within breathing distance of my Lady again, didn't i?"

"you don't belong to Her, so you don't have a say in a damned thing with regard to what i do and how i deal with Her."

"i see now that you're going to need to catch this fade i should have shot you yesterday. It's the only way you're gonna get right."

"you ain't old enough, boy, don't fuck with grown men until you're ready."

"Oh, i'm ready now, don't wait for me to grow up. Can't be held accountable for injuring an old head, that's not a good look. i wanna drop you while you're in your prime."

I couldn't get to the security teams quick enough, and there was no time to spare whatsoever. I had two men in a good, old-fashioned standoff, and it was only a matter of time before this whole situation turned into an utter explosion. This wasn't going to be the undercard at the next MMA pay-per-view, no matter how bad I wanted my ex-husband to catch those hands.

Under normal circumstances, I would have let this ride, but I couldn't let Goddess's event go to hell over this. Never mind the fact that lynx was the one who started this mess to begin with, but he'd gotten to the point to where he was more manipulative by the day. There was no point in saving someone who didn't want to be saved.

Still, I tried to exert some influence before they got there. "Jelani, he's not worth the trouble. Let him go so we can enjoy the party in peace."

"Yeah, Jelani, listen to the one you're pledged to for the weekend. From what i hear, it will be the last time you serve anyone for a little while." lynx glared at him, treating me like I wasn't even there. "I don't think you get it, but you will soon enough. Do what She tells you and do it for as long as possible."

"What you're going to do is be a good little fucktoy and leave before I deal with you." I stepped in his face, watching the smirk spread across his face. I knew that was what he wanted, but I was too far gone to care. "Away from here, know that I'll be dealing with you via any legal channel at My disposal. The fact that you won't adhere to a Top's request means you're the one unable to handle protocol."

"Please, no matter what You're doing "playing Domina", You will never get me out of Your system."

"you overestimate your worth to Me now. I've gotten you out of My system more than you know."

"Kitana—"

That merited a right cross that connected to his jaw, one with such force that the crowd erupted in a cascade of oohs. I didn't want to stop hitting him, even as he tried to readjust his jaw to see if it was broken. He sneered at me, recoiling when I raised my fist again for another strike.

"Oh, i see how this is gonna go…but that's okay, i promise

You that things are not done."

"Oh, they're done. They are so done."

Sigma was there within minutes, along with two of his regular detail. To say he wasn't thrilled was an understatement. He took assessment of lynx and Jelani and shook his head. "i'm going to need the two of you to stand down now, or i'll have no choice but to put you down. your choice."

Jelani wasn't hearing it. "i'm perfectly fine with that, but he's going down first, then you can do what you want from there."

Sigma stepped in front of Jelani as one of the other security officers secured lynx and carried him off. "Let us deal with him in the proper manner, don't get yourself hemmed up in the process. he's been warned to not approach my Lady anymore during this weekend or he would be removed from the compound, regardless of his Mistress. She was made aware and signed off on it within seconds."

Well, that changed the whole game for me. If it was that simple, I would have handled that in the first place. "Sigma, go ahead and take care of that for Me, please? And for that matter, I'll speak to the Council about a more permanent ban."

"To be honest, my Lady, You were better served to have done that before it got to this point," Sigma advised after the fact. "However, it is not my station to force anyone to do what they initially do not want to do. i am relieved, my Lady. he will not bother you again."

Once Sigma left the area, I gave Jelani a look that could have melted the coldest heart. I had to have him, point blank. I motioned for him to come closer, my eyes never leaving his the entire time. I didn't care that there were people watching us; it only intensified the emotions swirling inside me.

The moment he was close enough to touch, I placed my hand on his shoulder. With the slightest of movements, I dropped him to his knees. I slipped his head against my midriff, caressing his head and forcing his eyes upward to meet with mine.

"On Muva, that was the hottest shit I'd ever seen in my life!" tiger had to be the one to provide the light in what could have been a dark moment. "Girl, i didn't know You had that in You."

"That makes two of us." I heard Goddess's voice, which almost froze me in place. Even in Top space, she had the ability to hold me in place and take me captive. "For someone who wasn't comfortable with being on the left side of the slash, it looks like You took very good notes watching Me."

I wanted to giggle in response to that statement because it was all true, but with Jelani in his space at my feet, I had to maintain my discipline to keep the fantasy alive for him. "Yes, I had a great model to emulate."

"I kinda figured as much, sajira." The grin on her face was bright enough to blind any man who dared look in her face. It warmed me on levels that only she and Daddy would appreciate. "I loved watching You work, it was a proud moment for Me."

"Thank You, My Lady. It means a lot coming from You."

"Yeah, that was hot, Sis." shamise did her best not to disturb Jelani as he clung to my core. I swore that he was gonna get it the minute we were in my cottage. "What do You plan to do for an encore?"

I caught a glance of Mistress Blaze among the onlookers. The look on her face was pure disdain. I didn't care all that much; in my mind, she was dismissed, I didn't care what our stations would revert back to once the weekend was over. If my sis wanted an encore, I would give her an encore and make Blaze's head pop off from her body.

I pushed Jelani down on the ground, slipped over his body as I caressed his face. I could feel him growing under me, letting me know I was his in as complete a manner as could be had. A soft kiss across his lips turned into a deeper, more passionate interlude that made me want him to travel from France to Australia and have the whole world watch the journey.

A few seconds turned into several minutes. Silent commands between kisses had him molesting me in places that would make a high-end escort require an upgrade fee for the pleasure. I was lost in the moment, and there was no one to bring me out of it until I wanted to be. His body felt like it fit mine, the grooves sliding with a fluidity that threatened to intoxicate me beyond any point of return. I was at the point of wondering with legitimate curiosity as to why we were still here.

When we came out of it, the room was quiet. I had to look around—once my vision cleared—and make sure there were still people in the room. My eyes found Goddess again, along with a soft applause for the performance resounding from her hands. "Mmhmm, we will definitely need to debrief when we get done with this weekend. Okay, now that we've had our appetizer for the night, how about we get to the main course, yes?"

"Yes, My Lady, let's do exactly that."

"Wonderful." She turned to the rest of the crowd and popped off a series of loud claps to get their attention. "Nothing more to see here, folks. It's time to indulge and enjoy, the night is still young. Let's get to it."

Chapter Twenty-Eight

AMANI

"This is some bullshit! What point are you trying to prove???"

"The point we're proving? There is no point to prove, bruh. It's time to drop you off on the outskirts and make sure you never get back into the Golden City ever again."

The one thing that we never did was mess with the family in any way whatsoever.

It didn't matter if you were late to the party.

It didn't matter if you were there before the family was solidified.

It damn sure didn't matter if you were connected to an important branch of the family tree.

You mess with the family, you had to go. Period. Point blank. No room for ambiguity.

The penalty for messing with the family was simple: exile.

We all knew what this was, and there was no one who wasn't immune to that among us on the right side of the slash. Even those whom we serve and surrender to have the same code they had to abide by. If anyone violates the code, they risk the same fate.

Yes, it sounded like mafioso-level loyalty, but when you're dealing with a lifestyle that, whether we liked it or not, could get you arrested, fired from your occupation, problems with custody battles, and everything in between, you do what you had to do to inspire the concept of family.

That's what lynx found himself in the middle of dealing with. With Sigma standing in the corner because the cameras—well, let's say they were no longer a concern in this matter—observing at the request of Goddess in the event that there would be a need for a witness against the defendant. If I were him, I would be in fear of whatever it was that the three men in the room with me with ill-intentioned motivation had in store for me.

From the look on his face, he was beginning to gain an appreciation for the gravity of the situation he'd placed himself in. "Okay, look, maybe i took it a bit too far, but does it have to be all this? What do you think you're going to gain by doing this to me? The consequences could spell trouble for everyone in this room."

"And what do you think breaking and entering would look like for you?" Sigma mused as he continued to lean against the wall as an "innocent" bystander and witness. "your partner in crime already gave you up to avoid any type of criminal charges of her own. So, you have to ask yourself whether you truly believe you have the leverage that you think you do. Combine that flip with my Lady's statement that you were in Her cottage without permission, and i would say that you have a couple of different issues to worry about."

lynx tried to remain stone-faced until the reality of what Sigma explained began to seep in. He looked at tiger, realizing he was on the other side of the argument, leaving him in the singular minority. "Okay, so, now what? you just decide to rough me up and leave me outside to be collected?"

"Nah, this isn't how this is going to go, my dude." I looked over at tiger, who nodded in Jelani's direction in a silent consensus of what I was about to say next. "We figured it was best to have you speak with a higher power, since you decided the ones who were here were not worth the effort or respect."

The room we were in was one of the communications areas that Dom and Sigma used at times to interrogate when things went left on the compound. This room in particular had a large screen on the far wall that was used for specific situations. Once the screen activated, lynx found out the hard way why the Great One was what he was.

"Good evening, gentlemen. amari, how is everything going thus far, young'un?" Hearing my Sir's voice and seeing him on the screen was a welcome respite, considering everything we'd been dealing with.

"Everything is fine so far, Sir. We have had a couple of hiccups, but nothing that hasn't been handled without any real problems." I took a look at his surroundings, and it was a good guess that he was in the midst of resting from whatever they had to do that day. "There is, unfortunately, one who has been particularly belligerent, hence the reason for our setting up this video call with You."

"Considering the person sitting in the hot seat, I can understand why this request was made of Me." Sir seemed to refocus to speak to lynx, and from the frown on his face, it wasn't about to be a pleasant exchange. "Iceman, I don't know where things have gone wrong with you, but I believe we've reached the end of the line with you."

"my name is lynx now, Sir."

"you mistake Me for someone who gives a fuck, Ice. you know better than to try to correct Me when I'm speaking." Sir was in rare form, and I was ready for it all. "I know what's going on with you before you even know it, so don't pretend to think you are a step ahead of Me."

I watched him shut down after that show of force was met by the ultimate immovable object. I wasn't about to lie, I was in the midst of recording the whole exchange so I could play it later on. It would put the biggest smile on my sisters' faces. All I was going to do was sit back and watch him work, while taking notes at the same damn time.

"What has Me irritated more than anything is that I had to be contacted in the first place, which tells Me two things: you blatantly disregarded a standing order from a recognized Domina during this specialized weekend, and you did so with little regard for consequences or having the foresight as to how this would reflect on your former Mistress."

"Former Mistress? Sir, i believe You may be mistaken. The release was rescinded, which is why I was able to attend this event."

Ramesses chuckled a bit, which seemed to perturb lynx even more. He shook his head several times before he cleared his throat. "I love your penchant for assuming you have all the answers or that you're holding all the cards. Sin and I have already spoken at length about you, and you're done. As we've been chatting, all of your belongings have been shipped back to your old place. The fact that you thought you had the upper hand makes this even more laughable."

The dejected look on his face almost had me feeling sorry for him, and then I realized that I didn't care much, if at all. This was a long time coming for him. If anything, it will calm down a lot of unnecessary stress for sajira, it was pitiful that it had to come to bringing Sir into the mix to get to this point.

"That's not fair, She hasn't even heard my side of the story. How is She going to make a decision to release me without all of the facts?"

"What is going on with you, bruh? Did you suddenly begin working for the Trump administration and you didn't tell anyone?" His voice picked up its passion as he brought the whole conversation to an ending that only he could deliver. "your alternative facts on the situation have been refuted with hardcore numbers and camera angles that place you at the scene of several transgressions that your former Mistress could no longer bear."

His eyes widened as he realized the finality of it all. He tried to find the words to rebut what Sir said, but there was no getting around it. Mistress Sinsual would never allow him within shouting distance at this point. His shoulders slumped, and what fight he had left had been sapped from him.

"It's disappointing to say the least, and on top of that, not only will you have to deal with a restraining order due to your stalker behavior, but a permanent ban from NEBU, too."

"Now You're being unfair, Sir. i don't deserve a ban of any sort."

"It is in your best interest to take the L I'm giving you and roll with it, or do I need to remind you of the clause you've violated and the termination fee that's attached to it." Sir rubbed his fingers across his beard, the universal tell that he was measuring his words even greater care. "Consider it a final mercy from a former friend. I'm truly sorry that it had to come to this, but you signed your own removal papers. I wish you peace in your continued journey, if you are as authentic in your path as you have shown thus far."

"You're dropping me as a friend, too? We've been rocking for twenty years, Sir, and You're going to throw that all away?"

"Family over everything, bruh, and you're no longer family." Sir dropped the conversation cold after that. "amani, please get with Sigma and ensure that he is escorted from the compound and his access credentials are wiped from the system as soon as possible. By My count, you're doing this in the midst of a party sequence, and your designated Tops will be looking for you. Make this quick and quiet."

The screen went black, and effective ending to a frustrating period for all of us. I looked over at lynx, who looked like he'd lost his best friend. There was nothing more to do but to follow my Sir's directives, and do so with a smile on my face. Sure, it sounded cruel, but to be real, I didn't care if it did or not. I was glad I wasn't the target of my Sir's wrath. That's all that mattered to me.

Sigma picked lynx up to escort him to the cottage to watch him pack his effects and retrieve the membership credentials without another word. It felt anticlimactic as compared to what we wanted to do to him, but being disavowed by your best friend and cut off from the only kinky world you've known was worse than any physical pain we could have dished out.

Good riddance. Now I could go back to the party and cut loose without any further stressors.

Chapter Twenty-Nine

SHAMISE

Watching Jelani, amani, and Sigma walking up to greet Goddess, sajira and me felt like something out of a dream sequence. It didn't make any sense for that much exquisite fineness to be in close proximity to each other. It was all I could do to hold myself together as they closed the distance and began taking their respective positions at our feet.

Watching the debauchery while sitting with Goddess seemed to make everything right with the world. That balance, even in Top space, was hard to explain to the average kinkster who might not have quite understood how things work within our House dynamics. One thing was for certain: there was never a dull moment.

Taking a look around the space, I was happy Goddess decided on an open-air format. Between the pyrotechnics of the fire flogging in one corner of the space, to the waxing and fire wand play in a whole other section, to the good, old-fashioned spanking and rope rigging, it was a buffet feast for the senses. sajira and I kept sharing conspiratorial looks at each other, feeling like we were watching our own personal erotic movies play out in person.

But, as much as we wanted to enjoy the night on its merits as the highlight of the event, there was another reason we were all there at the same time. There was House business that needed to be conducted. It wasn't going to be pleasant, but we had to compare notes to figure out what needed to be dealt with in the morning before everyone departed.

"Goddess, everything seemed to roll pretty smoothly this weekend, for the most part." I began the initial conversation pieces before we eased into the crux of the matters at hand. "Everyone I've spoken to can't stop raving about the way things have gone."

"Yes, baby girl, things went pretty well, considering the other outside issues that needed to be addressed. In some cases, they will still need to be addressed." Goddess was in observance mode with Sigma, radios in hand in case the security detail needed to be alerted of anything that the dungeon monitor volunteers might have detected. "This last party for the night is really taking off into a whole other plateau. Sin is really wearing out the submissive we had to place in corrective protocol."

Sure enough, Mistress Sinsual was in her rare form, working over the politician that wanted to get back into Mistress Lohyna's good graces. Dude was in so many restrictive devices while being tortured that it made my head spin. Between the devices around his genitalia that would make any normal man flinch in pain, to the clover clamps and metallic clothespins that would have the average masochist jumping up and down with delight, there was no doubt that he'd learned his lesson with whatever he'd been put through before tonight's event.

"I can't believe the turnout tonight. I was half-expecting

people to retreat to their cottages and handle things behind closed doors before they had to return property to their rightful owners," sajira mentioned while caressing Jelani's head. She couldn't stop staring at him, and he was enthralled with her, which had me curious about what was going on between them in that moment. "I'll be happy when everything is over in the morning. At the risk of saying it in front of the boys, I miss My Goddess, dammit."

Goddess broke out laughing, enjoying the foot massage Sigma was providing her. "Sweetheart, this will be over soon enough, and You both have done very well. I'll have to be very creative with regard to what I need to do to get You back to Your normal selves. I think I have something in mind, but I'll wait until everything is handled first."

We didn't want to pout, considering we were supposed to still be in Top space, but she liked teasing us, and she knew that it was a trigger for us, too. It would be on our minds until it happened, and that torture alone would be enough to have us brat out the first chance we got. In her infinite wisdom, that might have been the whole point of her edging us like that.

Focusing on the task at hand, I noticed amani in a fit of uncontrollable laughter. He nudged Jelani and pointed in the direction of where the source of his laughter came from, and Jelani broke out laughing, too. I followed his eyes and saw a submissive being manhandled by two Dominas while he was tied down to a spanking bench. He was screaming out and begging for more torture as they continued to use every impact implement that they had available to them.

"Okay, you two, what's got you both so giggle happy that we need to be clued in on the joke?" I asked amani as he tried his best to calm himself. "It looks like he's having the time of his life. Is there something we missed?"

amani tried to stop laughing long enough to explain. He was still wiping tears from his eyes as he spoke. "i'm sorry, my Lady, but that dude claims himself a Pharaonic Lord Dominant and tried to come for me because i serve Sir and no self-respecting Pharaoh would ever be caught doing anything that would be an affront to his heterosexuality. Dude is getting ran through like a two-dollar hoe and had the nerve to try to call me on my shit?"

"Yeah, he was all "Pharaoh Lord Doms are righteous and masculine and all knowing" and would never be weak," Jelani chimed in. "So, to see him in the very position he swore he would never be in because a Domina put him there is karma at its finest. i'm just sorry we can't have cameras in open space right now."

The look on Goddess's face was priceless. "I need to screen the attendees better, but I should have known something wasn't right with him. he came with Lady Norene. And you're telling Me he said something against your Sir, baby boy?"

"Yes, Goddess. This dude tried it, only to have tiger shut him down and poke holes in the whole damn thing." amani broke out in laughter again as he continued to recount the events of that time. "Dude was on some "we recognize them, but they ain't a part of the Order, or some craziness like that.""

"I'm sure your Sir will be very interested to hear about that." Goddess's face conveyed her need to put that on her to-do list for the after-event meeting. "In the meantime, limit your interactions with him. I don't want him trying to rile you up any more than I assume he has."

"Yes, Goddess, i understand."

"And now that Norene has been brought up, I guess we

need to figure out what to do with Her," I segued the conversation to get to that issue, among others. "I don't know if You've been told, Goddess, but She tried to sway amani with some video of You and Sigma together. I guess She hasn't learned her lesson after all."

Goddess's eyes closed for a few moments, her body stiffening up as she digested what I'd disclosed. The minute she opened them, she looked down at Sigma, who nodded his head in agreement. "I figured She hadn't learned Her lesson, which is why I had Sigma dig up some stuff to bury Her. amani, did the video that She showed you show us outside of the main building when we were flirting and such?"

"Yes, Goddess."

"Beautiful. I have grounds to ban Her dumb ass from any event I have at any of the compounds." The smile on her face was a welcome sight, but I was confused over her calmer demeanor. The mere mention of Norene's name put her in a bad mood under normal circumstances. "Sigma, did we get the information from Mistress Ylana by satellite phone?"

"Yes, my Lady, She was most cooperative, especially when She found out about Norene's deception. She is looking forward to next year's event and wanted to extend Her apologies that Her schedule precluded Her from attending," Sigma replied. "She has already turned the information over to the local authorities for the information breach in her emails. Norene will be in for a lovely surprise when She returns to New York—Her and Her accomplice."

"Even better. There's no way to get out of this, I don't care what She tries to say to weasel out of it." Goddess looked elated, but moments later, her expression turned pensive. "I just wish I could be this happy about what I'll have to do with

Blaze. That one is going to hurt."

"What do You mean?" sajira asked.

"I can't disclose that, baby girl. Even though You're both in Top space, this will unfortunately be a private matter that eventually go public, but She put Herself in this situation." I could feel the sadness overcome her, but she did her best to mask it in the interests of dealing with all of the people who were interacting with us throughout the conversation. "Just know that it will be handled."

"Understood, Goddess."

In the next moment, Goddess's switch flipped, and she was back to her old self. "Enough of the business, it's time to have some fun! Get to it, and I'll check in with you tomorrow evening so we can decompress."

Chapter Thirty

NEFERTERRI

He stood before me, naked, in the wrist and ankle cuffs I'd placed on him, watching his body sway while attached to the Cross. His body looked even better without clothing, the heat of the night causing a slight sheen against his chocolatey skin. I did my best to keep my urges in check for as long as I could, but I knew it wouldn't be long before I gave in.

I walked around him, pinching his nipples and sliding my hands across his ass, giving light smacks to let him know I was right there in space with him. This was needed; we'd been working so hard the entire weekend, and tonight was for us to blow out every bit of steam we'd built up all weekend. He'd been edging me the whole time, trying to get away with different looks and slick phrases that were meant to get me to do something about it.

There was nothing to save him from what I had plans for.

He trembled a bit as I worked my fingers over his skin, noticing the goose bumps all over the muscles on his arms and chest. I licked my lips as the anticipation of what was to come began to consume us. *Mmm, he's not cold, that's for damn sure. I wonder what else I can do to make him quiver.*

The mood of a good scene was everything. When the foreplay had been building over the past forty-eight hours, there was no need to waste any more time. The tone was firm, but punishing. Fierce but compassionate. I sought my own redemption through his pain, my own spiritual release through my sadistic proclivities.

I stood behind him, raking my nails down his back, smiling as his body reacted. I cupped my hands over both cheeks, reaching around to grip his growing girth and deeming it more than adequate for what I wanted. A satisfied sigh escaped my lips as my body began to heat up beyond the point of any cognitive thought.

The grunt that came from Sigma aroused my inner primal predator. I growled in his ear in response, letting him know that he belonged to me tonight. There was nothing that would quell the intensifying conflagration boiling between us, and I had every intention of building his aggression to such a point to where, by the time I'd released him from his temporary shackles, the predator would become willing prey.

I began with the twin floggers, going from alternating strikes against his ass, moving to the back of his thighs, keeping a good rhythm between the two spaces on his flesh. I watched his body writhe and sway with each strike, a hypnotizing display that dared to lull me into a trance. I did my best to focus on where the falls on the floggers would land, fighting against the endorphin rush that might dull my senses.

His body was mine to use and abuse, to test its limits before I allowed it to be unleashed on mine. His groans amplified in my ears, causing my nether regions to moisten into a copious flood, causing my juices to trickle down my thighs. The torture I'd been inflicting was creating an unintended side effect: my body betrayed me on near biblical levels.

I kept up the pressure, watching his eyes close so he could, I presumed, absorb the harder strikes I was ready to inflict. That was nothing more than a silent challenge to do my worst, and I found the five-headed pinwheels to give a different sensation. I needed to bring him to the edge of animalistic desires. I wanted the beast within.

I pushed the spurs into his skin, causing a louder growl as he strained against the locks, resembling a caged wolf, intent on making its captor pay for daring to hold it against its will. I ignored the impassioned grunts and raked the spurs up and down his back, moving around his inner thighs, purring at his discomfort, beyond the capacity to care if he suffered. I wanted him to suffer.

"I know I'm reaching your limit, sexy, and I will move beyond it. I want to see the darkness you're hiding, I want to consume it. you deserve to let it loose, and I'm going to control every ounce of its essence." I heard the words coming from my lips, but it sounded like they were coming from someone else. It was an out-of-body experience that I couldn't quite explain, something that was indicative of the restraint I'd had to exert while ensuring that the event went off without a hitch.

I raked the pinwheels across his shaft, reaching the base and rolling them across his scrotum in as gentle a motion as I could. The prickly sensation was enough to bring him to that delicious place between pleasure and pain. Enough to drive him to the brink of sanity. I didn't want him to think, I wanted him to react.

"Give him to Me, sexy…bring Me the beast."

He looked at me, his eyes wild and raging, and I saw what I had been waiting to see. He was no longer the reserved and measured protector who'd kept me wet all weekend long. He was the wolf I wanted to devour every inch of me. I wanted the fight, to feel the aggression we'd both suppressed. But I wasn't about to make it easy for him.

The minute I released the cuffs from their locks, he'd pounced, dropping us to the floor. He reached for any piece of fabric to rip away to get at the prize he'd been kept from. He latched onto my nipples, causing a searing, pleasurable pain to course through my body. I pushed him away, matching his heat with my own need to grab and claw away at anything I could get my hands on.

I heard him sniff around my crotch, the scent of my arousal assailed his nostrils, sending him into a deeper frenzy. I flexed my quads as he tried to pry my thighs apart. I expected him to be able to overpower me, and I wasn't disappointed in the slightest as he'd succeeded in his initial conquest. I clamped my legs around him, making him lift me off the ground.

"Come and take it...if you can!" I challenged.

He grinned as he licked his lips, grabbing at my arms to pin me down against the plush carpeting. I moved my arms as quickly as I could to avoid his grasp, taking my nails and raking his chest in the process, further frustrating him. I tightened my grip around his waist, keeping my advantage until I felt the need to give up my positioning so we could consummate our scene.

He'd managed to wrangle his boxer briefs off his body, and I felt his shaft pressing against my thighs. I released my legs from his waist, keeping him at bay with my feet pressed hard against his chest. I frowned as I watched him try to reestablish his position between them. "Protection, now!"

He stopped in his tracks and retrieved the condom in the

next few seconds, slipped the covering over his weapon and found himself getting pounced on the minute he was in the proper gear to be handled and ridden within an inch of his life.

I clamped my hands around his wrists this time, gyrating my hips, claiming my prey as his eyes widened. The surprised look on his face was due to my ability to hold him down as I lay siege to his impressive phallic offering. I closed my eyes, focusing on my growing explosion rising from within my core.

He tried to match my strokes, wanting to please me in the midst of me taking control of his body and making it my personal amusement park ride. I found myself in a zone, feeling an intimate connection with my sex to the point to where it felt like we were one and the same. Nothing else mattered but my pleasure. Nothing.

I heard him groan and growl, feeling his thighs tightening, but I wasn't ready for him to erupt yet. "Don't you dare come! I'll get up right now and make you finish Me a different way, dammit!"

His eyes narrowed as he slipped out of my grip and grabbed my hips. The next thing I knew, I was being lifted off the ground, feeling the upward piston-action pumping of his shaft inside of my slickened yoni. The feeling was amazing; for a few moments, I felt like I was being held in suspended space while having no choice but to receive what I was being given.

My orgasm was imminent, and I had no time to speak its arrival. What resonated against the walls was high-pitched scream that seemed to reverberate all over the room. My body ignited, and the waves continued to roll and crash, leaving me little room to catch my breath. I yelled for him to put me down, needing to feel the carpeted floor to keep from feeling like I was in a dream sequence.

I felt my body convulse, going through the aftershocks of post-orgasmic bliss. I didn't know how he'd managed to have the strength to do it, but I felt the warmth of the aftercare blanket wrapping around my naked body. A pillow was placed under my head to make me comfortable, and I felt him as he tried to breathe deep in an attempt to recover from our interlude.

In the next moment, I felt my body being lifted from the floor and carried the short distance to the bed. My eyes were still glassy and I had a hard time focusing, doing my best to shake through the blurry vision I was experiencing. That proved futile, resigning me to close my eyes to focus more on breathing slower and calming my body.

"i'm happy i was able to please You, my Lady. It was an exquisite pleasure to have been in Your service," I heard Sigma saying to me. "May i be released from Your service to check on the rest of the compounds, to ensure that all protocols are still in place?"

I still had no voice. I could only manage a nod of my head to release him to continue to do what he was there to do— protect the compound and the attendees therein.

"Thank you, my Lady. i will have slave tiger come in and see to Your aftercare." He took my hand and kissed the back of my palm, his last gentleman's gesture before he left the room.

I did my best to sit up in the bed, taking the blanket to consume my body whole, awaiting tiger's entry with the usual list of things I needed to rehydrate and come down from a high that was all too familiar and welcomed with the comfort of a warm summer night.

As delightful as tonight was, I knew that it would be short-lived. I would have plenty of time to reminisce afterward, but there was still a bit of business to conclude first. There would be a reckoning on the horizon, and I would have no choice but to be its harbinger.

Chapter Thirty-One

AMANI

Waking up in bed with my sis felt like normalcy for me. To be real, I was used to sleeping with both my sisters, but sajira was still entwined with Jelani until it was time to go through the release protocol to end the event. Even with her being in Top space, it didn't change the intimacy between us.

It was a bit bittersweet that we would all have to go back to being on the right side of the slash. It was fun for a little while seeing them as Tops, but good things must sometimes come to an end. The fact that I still had them as part of my D/s family was more than enough for me.

I felt her stirring as my head still lay across her legs, and I lifted to give her time to stretch and wake up. She looked at me and caressed my face almost by instinct, a sleepy smile spread across her face. "Hi, baby, did you sleep well?"

"i was about to ask You the same thing, my Lady." I stayed in protocol for as long as possible, wanting to stretch things out in a selfish attempt to indulge my service fetish. "Can i get You anything? Is there anything You require?"

"Mmm, you can give Me a rubdown after the workout we went through last night." The mischievous grin on her face reminded me of the carnal activities we engaged in last night, riding the contact high of the scenes and sounds that played out in front of us. "Hopefully while you're doing that, we can figure out how to help Goddess with the madness swirling around Lady Norene."

I wasn't looking forward to dealing with that at all, but there wasn't much of a choice in the matter. I hadn't put much thought into it, and I had hoped that the situation would somehow resolve itself. It wasn't a matter of not wanting to confront it head on, but it was more of a matter of I wasn't sure if I would be able to contain my anger and want to forgo my training and discipline and tear through her like no tomorrow.

"Honestly, my Lady, i think Lady Norene has already signed Her walking papers, if what Sigma says is true," I remarked. "Did You hear what he said about the charges last night?"

"Yes, baby, I heard him, and I'm hopeful that those charges stick." She sounded a bit skeptical, more than I was used to. "The thing that gets Me is, how in the world did it manage to take so long? I know IT protocols take time to run through, but it feels like it could have come down sooner."

"my Lady, i'm of the mindset that, as long as we have the end result we want, it doesn't matter if it happened later rather than sooner. It happened before She could go back to New York and spin this like it was Goddess's fault."

"you have a point, baby boy, and I'll consider a win a win and enjoy the way this will go down later."

I kept the massage from getting too sensual, focusing more on the sore muscles so she could move and function once we got to the great room. They hadn't been moving like submissives since Thursday afternoon, so those muscles would feel brand new to them. I made a mental note to work sajira over once I got in her space so she wouldn't feel so stiff while we're in our kneeling positions.

Her cell phone rang, and the ring tone let us know it was Goddess calling. She picked up the phone and put it on speaker so we could talk to her together. "Hi, Goddess!"

"Oh, Lord, you two would sound like you got a good night's sleep." Goddess giggled for a moment before getting to the reason for her call quick. "The release announcement is in the next fifteen minutes, and I will need you to help tiger and Jelani get things prepped for the Council hearing to deal with Lady Norene and Mistress Blaze."

"Yes, Goddess, we will be there and on time," shamise replied.

"Good, that makes Me happy. God knows I need every shred I can get before this all goes down."

"We will do whatever it takes to keep You flowing positive, Goddess," I made sure she understood that there was no way that we would allow her to burn too much energy without finding a way to keep her balanced out and able to handle such a heavy burden. "i'll make sure to keep Your water and fruit at the ready, and my sisters will back me up."

"I know, baby boy, and I appreciate the three of you more than you know. This weekend was more emotionally daunting than I gave it credit for. I miss you."

Hearing her say that was more than enough to make up for the three days of not being in her energy. I looked down at shamise, and she nodded and winked, almost reading my thoughts while we were in the flow of the conversation. Now, I couldn't wait to make short work of these two trifling situations.

"We miss You more. We can't wait to see You."

I tapped shamise's shoulder to let her know we were done. We needed to get there early so we could give Goddess as much energy and capacity as we could. The next few hours would be demanding.

I watched with a mix of anticipation and trepidation as the Council members took their seats at the table. Since Goddess was the one who had the grievance, she could not be a part of the final decision. That rested in the hands of paka, Lady Hatshepsut and Mistress Sinsual. I wasn't sure whether Lady Norene would object to Mistress Sinsual and paka due to their connection to Goddess, but their collective track records of being impartial was beyond reproach.

Still, she couldn't help herself. "I want to lodge My protest of this hearing on the grounds that the Council members have a connection to the Domina filing the grievance. Can I expect a degree of objectivity with the evidence presented?"

Mistress Sinsual scoffed at the implication. "I can promise You, Lady Norene, that the three of us will be able to do so, without any measure of prejudice against You. The determination is sent to the other Councils for review and verification, as to show no impropriety. This is a process that I would not expect You to be privy to, since You are not a Council member of any of the compounds. Are we clear, so that we may proceed?"

Lady Norene's face was stoic as she processed the information. I wanted to wipe that smug look off her face with every fiber of my being. sajira was sitting with us near where Goddess was in the opposing chair.

Mistress Sinsual seemed a bit irritated over Lady Norene's silence and lack of answer. "I don't like repeating Myself, Lady Norene. Are we clear?"

"Yes, Mistress Sinsual, we are clear. I will accept the final determination and verification of the determination, regardless of the verdict."

"Very good. Lady Neferterri, You may proceed."

Goddess gave the information that she had on Lady Norene for the Council to read through. The look she gave Lady Norene felt like that woman might combust from the heat of her stare. "Members of the Council, it has come to My attention that Lady Norene and her accomplice, karimi El, conspired to commit fraud by doctoring the emailed information to Mistress Ylana with regard to attending this event."

"I object to these baseless accusations," Lady Norene interrupted. "You all saw the correspondence was legitimate between Myself and Mistress Ylana. Did You at least get in touch with Her to confirm that She transferred Her registration to Me?"

"Yes, Lady Norene, Lady Neferterri did get in touch with Mistress Ylana." paka continued to read through the information in front of her before she continued her statement. "According to the recorded conversation, She has not only accused You of illegally accessing Her email account, She has taken her accusations to the local police department. There is currently a bench warrant for Your arrest as we speak with the Nassau County Police Department."

"She's lying! I did not hack Her emails whatsoever! I spent money to attend the event, I have receipts!" Lady Norene was in full-fledged defensive positioning. "You confirmed those receipts! What kind of mockery is this?"

Lady Hatshepsut took her time to address the rebuttal. "Lady Norene, while we were able to confirm, based on the receipts You provided, and Lady Neferterri confirmed there was a glitch with the accounting firm that helped with the registration process with regard to Your registrations, we were, however, able to complete a forensics investigation, using funds to ensure impartiality. They were unable to find a payment from You for Your charge, karimi El, nor could they find one in his legal name, either."

Lady Norene's face turned bright red, and she looked like she was about to have a stroke. I was there for all of it and then some. "I demand to see this information! I don't believe any of you right now!"

"You're more than welcome to take the information with You as You travel back to New York, Lady Norene, but the information has been verified and notarized." paka did her best to not sound hostile as she took the liberty of delivering the death knell. "It is the determination of the NEBU Council that Your membership to all compounds be cancelled, and the termination fee that You consented to when You signed the membership agreement will be withdrawn from the bank account that You designated. We wish You peace in Your journey, and traveling mercies to face the charges that await You."

"You'll be hearing from My lawyer when I get all of this straightened out. I'll make sure You all pay dearly for this!" Lady Norene stormed out of the room, leaving the rest of us to figure out the pieces that needed to be cleared up.

Goddess looked around, wondering why it didn't last longer than what she'd planned for. "That felt...anticlimactic.

I honestly thought She would put up a bigger fight."

"Ma'am, i believe the formal charges in New York might have taken precedence," paka observed, doing her best to mask the smirk on her face. "Especially considering Her charge left Her holding the proverbial bag."

We were all a bit confused over what she meant by her last statement. Goddess asked for clarification, causing paka to straighten her face to provide the missing information.

"Before we arrived for this hearing, we'd gotten word that karimi El had secured a Lyft vehicle to head to the airport without telling Lady Norene," she recounted. "It might be safe to say that he might have been tipped off about the charges and felt like he needed to put as much distance between him and Lady Norene as possible, perhaps to try to cut a deal so he won't be punished too harshly."

"At this point, it is no longer in My circle of concern." Goddess was still in business mode, and everyone in the room could feel it. "We have one more bit of business to close out, and once that's done, I'm taking a couple of weeks to detox from all of this."

Chapter Thirty-Two

SHAMISE

"You betrayed the two women who had Your back for ten years, Blaze. Why in the world would You do that?"

"It won't matter why I did it, You won't see that You had a hand in all of this, Neferterri. Neither of You will."

"Enlighten Me, because I'm really confused right now over why we're catching all this heat from You."

Goddess was right, this would be the more emotional, more informal of the two situations that we needed to deal with. I didn't think there would be anything that we would be able to do to prepare for the anger that was coming for her and Mistress Sinsual. If anything, I almost felt like not being in the room and let them handle all that amongst themselves.

Sometimes, in dealing with matters that affected the family, the tough conversations had to be made.

Mistress Blaze's glare came in our direction, and in following her eyes, we realized she was staring at Jelani and amani. Her frown deepened, the lines in her forehead becoming more pronounced when she did that. "It's funny how they look so good together, now that I'm looking at them side by side. If I had the ability to turn back the clock, things might have been so much different."

"What in the hell are You getting at, Blaze?" Mistress Sinsual did her best to keep her cool, but there was only so long that was going to stay that way. "You're beginning to sound like a raving nut. You had Jelani, until You decided to release him in the middle of the damn event. How is that decision on either of us?"

"Because amani should have been Mine!" Mistress Blaze didn't waste any time letting her most authentic and rawest emotions and thoughts out for public consumption. "We had a freaking conversation about amani before Neferterri ever entered into the picture. I was supposed to have him, and You decided that Your *bestie* was more deserving than I was."

The whole room got quiet. Jelani looked at amani, a desperate need for an answer to help him make sense of what happened to him. amani's expression and mock surrender as he mouthed the words "I don't know" as we all looked back at Mistress Blaze to figure out what she was referring to.

"What? I never promised amani to You at all," Mistress Sinsual protested. "I remember talking to You about a few submissives, but You're developing a horrible case of selective amnesia right now, Sis."

"No, I think You're the one who got it wrong." Blaze's body language conveyed the hostility that boiled over and was directed at Goddess in particular. "You showed Me the pictures of amani—he was still Damien at the time—and I told You I wanted him for Me, since I was in the midst of releasing My last slave."

"See, now You're just spitting revisionist history, Blaze." Mistress Sinsual looked over at tiger, who was looking disgusted at what he was hearing. "Do You remember My tiger being in the room with us when this conversation took place?"

"tiger wasn't there for this conversation, Sin."

"My tiger is *always* there for any conversations I have when it comes to different slaves or submissives who come across My radar," Mistress Sinsual corrected. She was getting more animated by the second. "The reason he is always there is simple: he is My backup tape, in case things get either lost in translation or omitted completely."

"What I want to know are three things. First, why did You release Jelani? Second, why did You come for My amani with the intent of claiming him? And third, why did You then decide to set Your sights on lynx, knowing that he was still under Sin's consideration?" Goddess was trying to find a word in edgewise, considering she was the one being accused of usurping another Domina with regard to property. "I don't get it. Sin introduced Me to Damien the night of the party, and She said nothing about You inquiring about him. If I had known, I would have never gotten in the way of that."

"Yeah, that's really convenient, Neferterri." Mistress Blaze was still heated. "Imagine Me, knowing that there was a submissive that was supposed to be coming to meet Me at the party that night, and then imagine Me with egg on My face when he comes up to You, asking if he could be of service to You."

"This is getting ridiculous, Blaze, and You know it." Mistress Sinsual rubbed her forehead, trying to track her mind back to that sequence of events a couple of years ago. "The slave I was referring to during the conversation You're throwing in My face was not amani, it was another young man who'd just moved into Atlanta and found My profile on

FetLife and sent a message."

"No, You're twisting things up. It was Damien we were talking about."

"Blaze, oh my God, You can't be this serious right now?" Mistress Sinsual went through the conversations in her head, trying to find the conversation in particular that they'd had. She snapped her fingers after she happened to have a lightbulb moment. "I couldn't offer Damien to You because he was too young for You. You said so Yourself; You wouldn't consider anyone under 35 because You were against any "youngsters" that You would end up having to teach."

Goddess snapped her fingers, almost having her own lightbulb moment. "Blaze, You even told Me that he wasn't Your type because he was too young for You. How in the world are You gonna spin this two years later and say that we screwed You over?"

Mistress Sinsual looked at amani, bringing him into the conversation. "amani, love, when we talked by phone the night before the party here at NEBU, who did I tell you was interested in you?"

"Master Ramesses, my Lady," I answered without hesitation. "In fact, the reason that stuck out was because i asked why a Male Dominant would inquire about me. You responded that it was His wife who would be primarily interested in me, but that i would be providing non-sexual service for Him."

"You know what? It doesn't matter anymore." Blaze shook her head, incredulous over how this conversation was turning out. "I still got what I wanted in the end. lynx has agreed to rescind Your consideration status to be Mine. I didn't break protocol with regard to him."

"But You did break the honor code between the three of us, and that's just the tip of the iceberg," Goddess was heated. "You came for Mine, tried to sway him. You released a submissive who had been nothing less than stellar for You. You accused Me of impropriety during the Marketplace session. How in the world are we supposed to trust You?

"It's obvious that I no longer care what You think, either of You." Mistress Blaze leaned against one of the tables, refusing to sit through the entire conversation. "I'm done with the both of You, all that's left are the semantics of how this is going to dissolve."

"You selfish, self-righteous bitch." Mistress Sinsual began advancing toward Mistress Blaze. Jelani and I jumped to our feet, with Jelani holding Mistress Sinsual in place while I stayed in front of Mistress Blaze. "So, this is how You want this all to go down? Just like this? This is what we're going to do?"

"Yes we are." Mistress Blaze's response was laced with animosity. "So, what now? You wanna take a swing, Sin? I'd actually welcome it, it will help Me bury You even further into My past."

"I guess You wanted us to make this easier for You, so allow Me to do exactly that. Mistress Sinsual, I make the motion to permanently ban Mistress Blaze from all the compounds."

Mistress Sinsual didn't flinch, even while staring down Mistress Blaze. "I want this trick erased. I second the motion."

"Spare Me the dog and pony show, just get it over with." Blaze remained defiant, despite the fact that she wouldn't be able to access any of the compounds now. "If I'm banned, then I can leave, and You can have the termination fee while You're at it. This pitiful place needs all the money it can generate."

"Oh, You don't get to dictate anything, Blaze." Mistress Sinsual got in her face, almost ready to drop her with a left hook. "You have something that belongs to us."

"I don't have anything that belongs to either of You." Mistress Blaze was as aggressive in her stance as Mistress Sinsual was in hers. "I turned in My membership credentials before I even got here."

"That's all well and good, but what belongs to us is that ring on Your finger." Mistress Sinsual pointed at the signet ring that housed the crest of the *Nebet'new Nefrew Maa'kheru*, the organization that the Dominas created years ago. "You have been censured and removed from the organization, based on the violation of the tenets of the Ladies of Beauty and Honor."

I didn't know whether that was the straw that broke the camel's back, but one thing was clear: it broke Mistress Blaze's spirit. The tears began to fall, but she didn't say a single word. She looked down at the ring, admired it for a few seconds on her finger like she was trying to burn an image inside of her memory banks, and then took it off her finger. Instead of dropping it in Mistress Sinsual's hand, she dropped it on the ground and walked out of the room.

Mistress Sinsual didn't bother to pick it up. She motioned for tiger to grab a broom and dustpan from the kitchen. "It's worthless now, anyway, there's no need to do anything more than toss it out with the rest of the trash."

I was in shock over the way that this ended. I looked at sajira, and she couldn't speak, either. Looking over at Jelani and amani, and they were in as much disbelief as the rest of us.

All tiger did was comply with his Mistress's wishes and swept up the ring, taking it to the trash in the kitchen for disposal.

It all felt so…transactional, like the time that they'd spent together meant nothing at all in an instant. I wanted to say something, but the words escaped me on levels that I didn't know how to verbalize.

We, with Jelani in tow, walked over to both Dominas to give them the tightest hugs possible. I didn't know what else to do in that moment, and I wanted to cry for them for losing someone who'd been like an auntie to sajira, tiger and me.

There was an eerie quiet in the room for what felt like an eternity. It almost felt like an impromptu mourning period; even though Mistress Blaze wasn't deceased, the fact that her presence had been erased from our immediate existence made it feel like she was. There was no telling if we would ever cross paths with her again, whether at conferences outside of NEBU or anything like that.

It was simply…finished.

Chapter Thirty-Three

SAJIRA

We were going through the motions as we said goodbye to the attendees and watched them take their leave from the compound. Even the spectacle of Mistress Hera's exit wasn't enough to remove the pall from what transpired an hour earlier. If anything, watching everyone leave was a welcome relief, as it gave us the necessary time we needed to try and figure out what to do next.

Goddess still had the look of someone who'd lost one of her best friends. Who could blame her? She and Mistress Sinsual were going through the same thing, and there wasn't much that we could do about it.

We made our way back inside the main building once all the guests had gone, taking solace in the fact that the event was a huge success. Most of the attendees were excited to see if the dates would be locked in for next year so they could make plans, which would have been welcome news for Goddess. Hell, it would have put her on Cloud Nine.

Now, it didn't seem like it mattered all that much.

As we sat in the great room, I looked over at Goddess, determined to find a way to get her out of her mood. I dropped to my knees and crawled over to where she sat, almost forcing my way into her lap. A series of kisses all over her face seemed to bring her out of it as I felt the familiar grips on my hips.

"Hi, Goddess."

"Hi, baby girl. I guess you didn't want Goddess in Her feelings forever, didn't you?"

"No, Goddess, You know i don't like it when You're sad. i have to do something to make You smile, one way or another."

I looked down and saw amani, shamise and Jelani at the base of her feet, doing nothing more than providing a sort of protective barrier around where we sat. I imagined that it was a force field to keep the monsters from hurting Goddess, and it improved my mood in seconds. I looked at Jelani, and the second our eyes met, I knew I had to talk to Goddess about something important.

"Goddess?"

"Yes, My sajira, what is it?"

"You know i love You, right?"

"Yes, baby girl, I know you do. I also know that when you get like this, you're trying to butter Me up to ask something completely out of left field."

God, I hated when she could read me like that. I planted a few more kisses on her face until I saw her smiling again before I prepared my proposal. "Goddess, can we bring Jelani into the family? he's already kinda inside already when he was helping with the preparations for the event, and he and amani are already frat brothers, and i really like him and want him around more, and—"

"sajira, baby, slow down. I know how you get when you're really excited about something." Goddess did her best to indulge me, and I knew I could be a handful at times, but I didn't want him out of the loop. She looked over at a blushing Jelani, who was doing his best to figure out how he became the center of attention. "I have a feeling that you might have had this conversation with your sis and bro?"

"Well, no, not really, but i don't think they'd object to it." I looked over at shamise first, doing my best to send my thoughts telepathically, even though that wasn't a "thing". I looked over at amani, who was busy laughing at my attempts to pull this consensus without a single word to them. "i know they won't object to it, and it will balance the scales in the House. Isn't that what Daddy would say?"

"Wow, you pulled one of Daddy's favorite sayings, sis," shamise noted. She still couldn't contain her laughter, but I guessed she wanted to let me off the hook. "Goddess, i think i can speak for amani when we say we're good with it. Besides, this is the most animated sajira has ever been about anything."

amani nodded, placing a hand on Jelani's shoulder. "i mean, we're frat, so this just puts things on a closer perspective now. We really would be family if You and Sir sign off on it."

Goddess seemed to exhale slow and steady while I was still in her lap. I batted my eyes while she looked in mine, trying to find some semblance of sanity in them. I kept smiling, my eyes expressing themselves as they always did, intent on getting my way the best way I knew how. She started playing in my hair, caressing my face, and in that moment, I knew she'd made up her mind. It was a matter of convincing Daddy.

"Okay, baby girl, I'll talk to Daddy and see if He's on board with this."

My smile widened even more, and I hopped off her lap to grab at Jelani to hug him tight. "i can't wait until you're an official part of the family, baby. It's going to be fun!"

Jelani's eyes met mine, then shot to Goddess's, where they remained for a few more seconds as he took in the breadth of what I'd just proposed. "my Lady, are You sure? i mean, i'm not well-versed in D/s protocol and stuff like that."

"Don't worry about that right now, Jelani. I have a pretty good feeling that there will be three other people that will do their best to get you on the straight and narrow. Isn't that right, you three?" Goddess cut her eyes in our collective direction, her demeanor and body language giving us the silent clue that the onus will be on us to get him up to speed on House protocol if we wanted to keep him around.

Jelani bowed his head. "Thank you, my Lady. You and Sir will not regret this."

"I haven't had a chance to try to convince Him yet on the merits of owning another submissive, so don't thank Me quite yet," Goddess tapped the side of the chair as she rose from her seat. "But for now, you can stay in His good graces, sight unseen, by helping with the cleanup efforts. you may have a better leg to stand on when He gets back from His overseas trip."

"i understand, my Lady. i won't disappoint."

"Good boy, I like that. Now, the four of you can get to work, there's things I need to attend to some after-event affairs. We will reconnect in about two hours so I can get a gauge on your progress."

Epilogue

NEFERTERRI

Meeting my Beloved at Peachtree-DeKalb airport a couple days after the SAMOIS weekend was over was equal parts needed and wanted. I always missed him when he's gone, and the return always triggered heat wave warnings. This time around, however, I needed him to balance me out.

The past couple of days were cathartic in a sense. I went through a period of mourning the loss of a woman I once called sister, before realizing that things happened for a reason. Causality was something that couldn't be dismissed out of hand.

I had a chance to talk to Sin for the bulk of the day, and we had the opportunity to figure out where things could have possibly gone wrong with Blaze. In the midst of the conversation, a misunderstanding of epic proportions happened, all due to a miscommunication that could have been handled years ago.

Blaze's assumption was that, since she and Sin were friends for a longer period of time, she had the "default" when it came to any new male submissives that came into the personal universes of either of the three of us. That type of arrogance was beyond my comprehension. It wasn't amani that she felt that way about, either; lynx was supposed to have gone through her first, too.

I'd wished someone would have sent me the memo on that, so I could have crushed those dreams in a heartbeat. I didn't put myself in that elevated position, and I wasn't about to elevate anyone else to that status either. My properties may call me Goddess, but I didn't take myself so seriously that I expected other Dominas to defer to me and send me prospective property like I was owed tribute. This wasn't *Game of Thrones*, and I wasn't Cersei Lannister.

Seeing Beloved walking off the private jet with Amenhotep and Dominic gave me all sense of carnal lusting. He looked like a bronzed demigod, although he looked a bit tired, too. A near ten-hour flight would do that, I'd guessed.

As tired as he looked, it made my insides warm and gooey the moment his eyes lit up at the sight of his Beloved awaiting his arrival and looking at her like he still had enough energy to let me know how much he missed me. The minute he wrapped those long arms around me, I melted, and all my troubles melted away in an instant.

"Hey, You."

"Hey, You. How was the flight?"

"It was pretty smooth for the most part, we had to divert the flight pattern to avoid a few storms over the Atlantic, but once we got into US airspace it was all good." He still didn't take his hands off my ass as we talked. The concern in his eyes was evident; I could avoid them over video chat, but in person was a whole different matter. "Are You okay, Beloved? I mean, all things considered?"

Amenhotep popped up before I could answer the question,

but His first question for me was similar to Beloved's. "Now, You know I can't have My darling "daughter" frowning and such, that's not how this works. Are You okay, My dear?"

The first genuine smile popped across my face in the past two days the moment I heard His voice. No matter what the situation, His energy uplifted you, whether you wanted it to or not. "Yes, Father, I'm getting better by the day. It was a bit rough for a while there."

"I can imagine. Well, I'm glad that things are okay. I will leave You to Your Beloved." He made His way to the executive SUV that was also on the tarmac, where paka was waiting for Him. I watched Him disappear into the vehicle before it made for the exit, heading to take them down to Hartsfield-Jackson for the flight home.

Dominic was the next to greet me, his face showing the same concern, but realizing that Amenhotep had managed to erase the gloom from my face. "I'm happy that things went well, security wise, for Your event this weekend. Sigma tells Me that everything went off without a hitch and the volunteer personnel helped take some of the stress from our normal staff."

"Yes, Dom, everything was wonderful, and thank You for keeping My Beloved out of trouble down there in South America." I gave him a hug before pointing him in the direction of his truck, where I knew Natasha and Niki were perched and waiting for him. "I know how fluent He is in Portuguese, and I didn't need Him getting caught up down there."

"It's always a pleasure, My Lady. Now, if You will excuse Me, I have two girls who haven't seen Me in almost a week." Dominic turned on his heel to head to his truck. Niki and

Natasha exited the vehicle, waved to us from a distance, and embraced their Sir like he'd been gone on deployment.

Now that we were alone for a few moments, it gave me a chance to be nosey for a change. "So, how was Brazil? Were You able to secure the location You wanted?"

"Yeah, the old man got what He wanted." He shook his head before chuckling to himself. "I don't know how He manages to do it, but He always finds a way to teach Me something."

"That's what good Fathers do, Beloved. The lessons never stop coming, even when You think they have." I hugged him again as we headed to our SUV to head home. Once we slipped inside, I continued my query. "So, what type of event format are You conjuring up this time, and why is it not a good idea that Me or Sin or any Domina attend said event?"

He smirked as he stroked his chin. I already knew it was something I didn't want to know about at that point, I just wanted to ensure that our girls were not being placed in harm's way. "Beloved, all I can tell You is this: the women who decide to enter into this fantasy weekend will have to pledge allegiance to the Code, the whole Code, and nothing but the Code."

Unthinkable

RELEASE DATE: MAY 15, 2018

Devin

Chapter One: When a Woman's Fed Up

"It's over. I can't do this anymore."

I looked at the phone like it would infect me with an incurable disease. "What do you mean, it's over?"

"I need something different, Devin," she explained. "What we had was good, but we want different things now."

The voice over the phone, the one that only a week ago sang in high octaves to any deity who would listen over how much she loved me while I was digging in her yoni, now sounded like poison, making my ears bleed.

"You're really serious? Yeah, this is a joke," I spat. "You want to make me beg to keep you and what we have or something? Yeah, that's it, that's got to be it."

"Don't make this harder than it has to be," she pleaded over the phone. I ignored the way her voice cracked, like she wanted to play to my sympathies. She was the one who wanted to end things, not me, the fuck did I look like being sympathetic. "I'm not the woman that I was a couple of years ago when we met. Our dreams are different now. The paths that we're taking are, too."

There was no doubt in my mind where this conversation was headed. She wanted to throw the "marriage and kids" thing in my face again. We'd been arguing about that the last few weeks, but it seemed like she was almost adamant about it over the past few days, nearly popping off an ultimatum. I didn't know what was worse: having this conversation yet again or facing the inevitable demise of this relationship, and the waste of two good years of my life.

As I listened to her drone on about her so-called evolution, it dawned on me that things had gone way deeper than I'd originally thought. She'd upgraded me, I felt it in her tone. She thought she wanted to let me down easy, but in reality, she could have easily dropped me off a cliff and it would hurt the same way.

"I know this isn't easy, but hopefully we can still be friends, baby." Her voice was calm, but I didn't want to be. She had the audacity to come out of her mouth with the "let's be friends" part of the break-up conversation. "It doesn't have to be bad between us, baby."

Friends? Really? No thanks, not in this lifetime. That was the final straw. I ain't nobody's emergency option in case things didn't go well with the upgrade. She was not taking any more power from me.

"You're right, this is over, and no, we can't be friends." I felt the need to regain some semblance of dignity, despite the fact that my heart was breaking. She was not about to hold any power over me. "And don't call me baby, you've lost that right. In fact, lose my number and don't call me anymore."

That conversation happened about three months ago.

Oh well, shit happens, but this type of shit didn't happen to me. I'm Devin Lowery, goddammit.

Still, how could I have been so blind? I mean, she sent all the signals:

The new provocative clothes and lingerie…

Going out to the club with the girls…at least that's what she told me…

The change in her sexual appetite…I mean, she became something completely different before my eyes, asking me to do things that we'd never even talked about before. The funny thing was that we'd already been engaging in some kinky play, with her taking a more submissive role in our sexual play, but she'd been trying me, being more aggressive and combative toward the end. That should have given me the clue that she'd been cheating on me.

All the signs were there, but I didn't see it coming…or, more to the point, I didn't *want* to see it coming. If I'd stuck to the rules and stayed on my game, I wouldn't be sitting here looking stupid, but my nose was too wide open, thinking she was the "one". Under normal circumstances, my instincts would have been hypersensitive enough to warn me of the impending blindside hit.

I looked back on everything I'd done, all the sacrifices I made for this relationship, more than my fair share. But I guess that wasn't enough for her. That's what I got for ignoring my base instincts and letting her get inside so deep that I couldn't tell which way was up.

The one thing that gnawed at me was a decision that would have stunted my growth if I wasn't associated with my employer. I gave up big money about a year ago, turning down some overseas photo shoots that would have made me a superstar in the fashion industry. Being an up-and-coming photographer, turning down jobs wasn't an option unless there was a damn good reason. I thought that she was that damn good reason.

That was my first strike.

Hindsight was 20/20, with the laser focus of an FBI sharpshooter.

Thankfully, it didn't kill my career, and I was able to parlay my skills to eventually become one of the most sought-after video producers in the industry, with the prospect of being able to be the next Ryan Coogler, especially now that he's got *Black Panther* trending so hot that it has the whole industry buzzing on a whole other frequency. *That* was where I wanted to be, and *that* was where I was going to be. Thanks to the filmography classes I took at USC when I was younger, I might be well on my way to doing exactly that, especially now that I was situated in "Hollywood South".

I should have known she was pulling away from me, but I had fallen victim to the spell that love had cast over my heart...a heart I thought I'd protected. Cupid's a dead motherfucker, God as my witness.

Being the logical thinker that I was, I had to be honest with myself and check my own ego at the door. Maybe I set myself up for this fall. After all, I had my rules, and my number one rule was to never fall in love until they fell in love with you.

I thought I had that rule covered...boy, was I wrong. But, that's what I got for thinking I had all my bases covered.

Okay, so I wasn't entirely innocent. I mean, who jumps out of a plane without a parachute? I kept a few women who were still in my corner, and some continued to make passes at me, despite my relationship. But all of them knew who she was, and for the most part, they were okay with that. If I was totally honest with myself, then it might have been Karma knocking down the door to make me pay for not being "all in" with the relationship I was in. I could have waxed philosophical for the next few days playing the "what if" game, but frankly, I no longer cared. As far I was concerned, my game was still on point; I allowed my feelings to get in the way. It was her loss, regardless of whether I thought she was worth letting all of the side pieces fade to black in order to make her the center of my universe.

The moral of this story? Never make someone a priority when they saw you as nothing more than an option. The problem with that moral was that I didn't make sure I was not an option.

That was my second strike.

There was no room for strike three because I got tossed out of the game for arguing the call.

Jenna Whitmore was everything that I thought I wanted in a woman: ambitious, aggressive in her business dealings, sensual to a point to where she could have any man eating out of the palm of her hand. She knew what she wanted, and she knew how she was gonna get it. She had the type of drive that made me want to match hers tit-for-tat, and the way my life was set up in that moment, I needed someone who fit what I needed from my woman.

Despite all the pros of the situation, she did have her downside; that damn hindsight thing again. She was never very affectionate away from the bedroom. She was nonchalant at times, and the words "I love you" didn't have the same effect as I thought they should have. I tried to convince myself that none of that mattered…I loved her, or at least I thought I did.

My friends and family had a fit when they found out. My best friends, Anton and Quinn, couldn't believe that I'd chosen Jenna in the first place. In their eyes, there were other women in my "harem" that were much better suited for me than Jenna. Natalia, my best female friend, never liked her, and looking back on it now I saw the reasons why.

I wasn't trying to hear any of them, though. I'd made my choice, I had to live with it, and that was what I told my friends and family. There was no point in going back on my word at this point, and I didn't have time to hear the "I told you so" speech from anyone.

Charge that shit to the game…and that's exactly what I did, too.

I made myself a promise that I wouldn't let my heart make any more decisions from now on…once it mended, of course. The chairman of the board would handle things for a while.

Ladies, if you don't know who the chairman of the board is, ask your man, or ask any man that you've been intimate with. Chances are, you've had more than a few conversations and "meetings" with him, and depending on that man, "he" went by many names. That's not important right now, what was important was getting through the mess I was dealing with at the moment.

It's funny how many times you hear the words "I told you so" when you screwed up. They came fast and furious, especially from my best friends, Anton and Quinn. Natalia, my closest female friend, gave me an earful, too, but once she saw how hurt I was over the whole thing, she softened her tone.

The noise was so deafening that I closed off from all of

them…well, almost all of them.

My older brother had my attention, and for real, why wouldn't he? In my mind, he had it all: great career, a fine-ass, intelligent, business-savvy wife, three beautiful kids, and a house in the upper middle-class section of Highland Park, not too far from Chicago, Illinois.

I thought that since he had made mostly the right choices, listening to his advice would get me to where he was at thirty-three years old. He even told me a few years ago that it would have been best to get the "Southern Playalistic" out of my system before I settled down, just like he did.

I thought I was ready at twenty-eight.

Unfortunately, the partner I thought I would be able to put those plans into motion with had plans of her own.

What was it they said about the best laid plans?

Oh well, it was time to start fresh, and since 2016 had come and gone and we were only a few days into the new year, now was as good a time as any.

"Yo, D, we heading to the Havana Club, you down?"

It was an unusually warm Saturday evening when Anton called me. He had the bright idea of rolling through the clubs downtown and midtown club circuits, since we both had the day off tomorrow. It figured he wanted to go out more now. He was in the midst of a bad dry spell and he'd picked up on my old habit of picking up a new bevy of beauties every few months or so, and this time of the year was prime feeding time.

At the beginning of the year, I usually scooped up around four or five women, depending on my mood and what I had a taste for, and let the war of attrition bear out who the weakest links were until one remained. I had no problems getting back to that plan, but there was no motivation anymore because I was still healing from losing Jenna.

I was too tired to have strength in numbers, no matter how much pleasure my body would enjoy, it would take too much out of me. Despite all of those reasons, I agreed to go with Anton, but if anything hit my radar, I decided I was going to be picky—*very* picky.

"Come on, Devin, I'll even come through in the Yukon and grab you. You ain't even gotta drive tonight. I got a sweet tooth for some chocolate, and Quinn's coming, too. It will be like old times, bruh." Anton made a very strong case, and I couldn't argue. I didn't have to drive, either? Man, listen.

"I'm down, bruh, I'll see you at my place in thirty."

"All right, bet. See you in thirty."

I hung up the phone and my mind began to think back to what my father told me when I was in high school and I lost my first love.

My father was old school, last of a dying breed of players from the sixties and seventies. You know the ones that had a "mistress" that the wife knew about, but as long as he was taking care of home, the wife didn't care too much about who else he was fucking with.

He saw me trying to look like I wasn't crying in my bedroom after the "love of my life" decided that she wanted to be friends.

"Son, it only takes thirty seconds to get over a girl." I could still hear him laughing as he said it. I didn't find it so funny since my heart was hurting as much as it as. "You lose one, pick up a few more. It ain't nothing like new pussy to help you forget."

I took that lesson and ran with it for as long as my heart and body would let me. For a while, it worked, and I didn't have to worry about my heart being broken until I felt like I wanted to bother with putting it out there to be broken again.

Pops said it took thirty seconds.

Well, it took a lot longer than thirty seconds…a lot longer. Jenna was not some random chick on the street that I'd been playing around with. She was supposed to be my forever. This one was going to take a long time to get over.

But like he told me, the best way to forget about the last one is to pick up on the next one.

One thing was still for certain…even if I could forget about the last one, it still hurt like hell.

ABOUT THE AUTHOR

Shakir Rashaan is the bestselling author of the *Nubian Underworld* series, the *Kink, P.I.* series, and *In Service to the Senator*. His other projects include upcoming releases *Unthinkable* and *The Devil's All-American*. Other projects are in development for later publication under P.K. Rashaan. If you want to read more, visit www.ShakirRashaan.com.